THE

AMARA

CHRONICLES

Frank Williams

Capriarc Press, Mesilla, New Mexico, USA

Capriarc Press

331 Capri Arc, Las Cruces, NM 88005

ISBN: 978-0-578-02178-2

To Madeleine and Miranda

Chronicle the First

Amara and the Watervoices

Chapter One.

*T*he river flows out of the desert, bringing melted snows from distant mountain ranges. It widens as it nears the city. In moonlight, the desert breeze forms intricate patterns of reflections on the surface of the water. But when the moon is low and the night is dark, there are a small number of gifted people who can see a glow coming from within the water. Among those, an even smaller number can listen carefully and hear the music of watervoices and the words of their song. The voices sing of the past, of the present, and of that which is yet to come. Before they sing the future into their song, there are infinite possibilities. But once the watervoices foretell what is to happen, the future can never change.

*

Eleven-year-old Amara tossed back and forth on her bed of straw. She was not sleeping well on this sultry evening. Balarta, capital city of the kingdom of Weltoria, was sweltering in summer heat. The outskirts of Balarta, where Amara's family had its hut, was on the edge of irrigated fields and seemed to suffer the worst. Perspiration dripped from her face and humidity pressed against her from all sides. She stared upward and listened to the flies buzzing in the darkness overhead. It was no use trying to sleep. She pushed herself upright and left the hut. Even outside, the heat was oppressive, so she wandered to the riverbank in search of cooler air. As she stretched out in tall grass next to the water, welcoming the feel of the breeze on her skin, she heard the eerie music of watervoices coming from the river.

In a tower high above the city, Maleviol, the king's First Minister, was pacing to and fro on a balcony. Below him, temple spires, housetops, and narrow streets stretched from the palace down to the river. The warm evening breeze stirred his robes but he did not notice.

Important affairs required his full attention, too important to permit him to look for the glow of the river and listen for the music of the watervoices. In two nights the events would begin that would put into action his years of planning and waiting. He ached to see the blood of his enemy flow. For now, he stood quietly, waiting for the bells to sound the third hour after midnight, the appointed time for the meeting of his cabal.

In another tower, across the palace, the king slept unsuspectingly in his chambers, protected by his ferociously loyal, never-sleeping guardians, the Watchful Ones.

Far below, in the heart of the city, Shadenni, a grayish-yellow tiger cat, chased a lizard across a tiled roof and into an open window.

Amara lay sleepily in the grass next to the river and listened to the music of the watervoices. Their gentle sound lulled her almost to sleep before she realized the ominous message they were singing.

Two nights from now, two nights from now, the king will not sleep.
Two nights from now, the best in the land, their trust will not keep.

Amara knew that the prophecies of the watervoices always came true. She was one of those who had the gift of hearing them, so she listened closely to see what the voices would tell her.

Two nights from now, two nights from now, evil will talk.
Two nights from now, among the high, danger will walk.

She puzzled over the meaning of the song. Treason in high places? The king in danger? Wide-awake now, she hurried back to the hut, wondering what to do.

Across the city, Amara's uncle, Rabak the thief, held his breath, keeping his pudgy body motionless and flat against the wall in a house that was not his own. Moments passed, then the cat Shadenni, chasing the lizard, jumped onto the windowsill and Rabak relaxed. Moving quietly, he lifted himself and his bag of purloined valuables to the window, gently dropped the eight feet to the alleyway below, and disappeared into the night, moving silently through the dark streets past shuttered houses.

Back in the palace, Maleviol closed the door after the others had entered the darkened chamber. He wrapped his silver robes tightly around him and ran his fingers through his bushy black beard. The plotters gathered closely while he reviewed the outline of his plan.

He pointed to one of his men. "Satriz, in two nights, at two bells past midnight, your men will make loud noises in the hall outside the king's chamber, diverting the Watchful Ones who guard the door."

He faced another hooded form. "Olyah, your group will enter the chamber and fire the smoke flares, eliminating all visibility. Quickly, before the king can invoke the magical powers at his command, you will slay him and remove his body from the chamber."

He continued, "At great difficulty I have been able to obtain a powerful enchantment. Namintor will take the king's place in bed, surrounded by the enchantment which will give him the appearance and the powers of the king. He will summon the Watchful Ones back into the bedchamber. Satriz and Olyah will carry the king's body to our mountain fortress and dispose of his remains where they will never be found. Namintor's enchantment will last for seven days, during which time he will turn over all power to me."

He looked around the room. "We will now go over detailed plans of each of your parts in the coup. We cannot risk even the smallest mistake."

At the edge of the city, Amara ran into the hot air of her family's hut and tried to wake her parents with her news. Her father, Taran, rolled over drowsily and told her to wait till morning. Her mother, Asuma, woke more easily. Amara pulled and tugged until both her parents agreed to go out to the river with her.

When they reached the riverbank, the voices were still singing their warning.

Two nights from now, two nights from now, the king will not sleep.
Two nights from now, the best in the land, their trust will not keep.
Two nights from now, two nights from now, evil will talk.
Two nights from now, among the high, danger will walk.

Amara's parents listened carefully. They could not hear the watervoices as clearly as Amara could, but they heard them well enough to realize that the king must be told.

"How can we warn him?" she asked.

"I don't know," answered her father. "They would never let peasants come near the king. Especially with a tale as hard to believe as this one."

Silence came as they thought over their problem.

"Let's ask my brother," said Asuma. "He is wise in the ways of the world."

Taran nodded his head. Surely Rabak, the famous and accomplished thief, would know how to gain access to the royal presence.

Rabak had just finished hiding his night's acquisitions and pulling a blanket over his head when Amara and her family ran into his house to tell him the prophecy of the watervoices.

"I will need to sleep before I can consider this matter," he said. "Tomorrow at midday I will take Amara to the palace walls. Perhaps a plan for warning the king will suggest itself."

Shadenni slept soundly in a sewer entrance, digesting the lizard.

The Watchful Ones maintained their vigil while the rest of the city still slumbered.

The first glimmerings of dawn began to light the city. Maleviol and his plotters left the tower and melted into the halls and passageways of the palace.

*

By the time the sun had passed its highest point, Rabak and Amara had become part of the bustling crowd in the market that surrounded the royal palace. Smells of grilled meats and fresh herbs filled the air. As Rabak pretended to bargain with an herb-seller, Amara saw him glancing up at an ancient waterspout whose outlet lay slightly more than one man's height above street level in a quiet corner of the palace walls.

Within the palace, the king and his ministers were finishing their midday meal and preparing for the afternoon's public audience. As always, the Watchful Ones had observed every step in the preparation of the king's food, and tasted every dish carefully before it was served to the king.

Shadenni lay napping in the sun outside the kitchen door of an inn, waiting hopefully for scraps of garbage to be thrown into the alley. As he waited, he took special note of the two peasants wandering through the market.

Rabak and Amara continued their circuit of the palace. When they heard the announcement of the beginning of the king's public audience, they tried to enter. Their way was barred by a giant doorkeeper. "Keep moving, you two! The king's audiences are for respectable landowners and merchants, not ragged peasants!"

"Please let us in," cried Amara. "It is important that we see the king."

"Nothing that such as you might say could be of the slightest importance to the king," thundered the doorkeeper.

She tried to run past the guard, crying, "Please, please!"

He pushed her roughly back into the street. Rabak touched her on the shoulder. "We must go," he murmured. "We need a better plan."

*

The sun went down, and lights went on throughout the city as darkness fell. When the moon dropped low in the night sky, Rabak and Amara returned to the riverbank. They waited patiently for the watervoices to sing. As the last traces of moonlight vanished from the sky, a faint shimmering light appeared under the water. As the glow grew brighter, the listeners began to hear the song.

One night from now, one night from now, the king will not sleep.
One night from now, the best in the land, their trust will not keep.
One night from now, one night from now, evil will talk.
One night from now, among the high, danger will walk.

Rabak and Amara went on listening. The voices told the story of the plot. They finished:

High in the castle, chamber covered with smoke,
But all can be saved, the plotters may choke.

Amara was worried. "We will never get into the palace. The walls are too strong and high. The king will never hear our warning."

Rabak pulled back his rounded shoulders, raised his shapeless body to its fullest height, and replied with as much dignity as he could muster, "I, Rabak, am the greatest thief in the world. No walls are too strong and high to keep me out."

They returned in silence to Amara's hut and slept until daybreak.

Chapter Two

Maleviol's men had difficulty concealing their excitement about the events the night would bring. There would be no public audience today for the king, so the traitors stayed within their chambers, storing up their energies.

Amara and Rabak took another tour of the palace walls. To a casual passerby, the walls would seem vertical and smooth. But as Rabak laughed and joked with rug dealers and spice merchants, his sharp eyes carefully observed tiny bumps and crevices in the portion of wall that lay above the waterspout he had noted the previous day. He then returned with Amara to sleep through the afternoon in her family's hut.

Amara's parents spent their usual day, working from early morning to late evening in the sweltering heat of the fields. Older peasants working around them marveled at Taran's strength and energy. They still remembered the delicate six-year-old boy who had been brought years before to be raised by a peasant family. He'd grown to become one of the hardest field-workers among them.

Shadenni spent his day scavenging for morsels of food dropped under the stalls at the market.

When sundown came, the king sat in his dining hall, enjoying the music of minstrels and the company of courtiers as he dined on his evening banquet.

*

Darkness fell over the city and one by one the lights in dwellings flickered out. Amara appeared at Rabak's house just as he was leaving for the palace.

"I'm coming with you," she said firmly.

"This will be difficult and dangerous," he told her. "No place for a little girl."

She looked up at him. "The watervoices spoke to me," she said. "I deserve the chance to help warn the king."

Rabak saw the determination in her eyes and reluctantly nodded his head. Amara joined him eagerly. They stole quietly through deserted streets and approached the palace walls. Shadenni noticed them and followed. This was the time for which he had long been waiting. Rabak picked up the cat and cradled it in his arms. It started purring as he scratched behind its ears.

"One never knows when one will need an ally," he told Amara.

"What will happen if we are caught in the palace before we see the king?" asked Amara.

"It is better not to think of that possibility," said Rabak. "The fate that awaits trespassers in the royal palace is not pleasant to contemplate."

The three of them arrived at the palace wall and stopped under the waterspout. Rabak put Shadenni down and lifted Amara over his head to the outlet. She crawled onto the pipe, and Rabak passed the cat up to her.

He launched his bulky body lightly from the ground, grabbed the edge of the spout, and pulled himself up. In the near-total darkness, he slowly disappeared up the sheer palace wall, using his fingers and toes to find the cracks and bumps he had memorized earlier.

He pulled himself over the top of the wall and lowered a silken rope with a loop in its end to Amara. She slipped the loop around her waist and let Rabak draw her and Shadenni up to him.

They dropped as quietly as possible inside the wall to a walkway used by palace guards. The two of them moved cautiously, but rounding a bend, they almost collided with one of the giant sentinels. He reached to grab Rabak, but his arms closed around emptiness. Rabak had ducked quickly behind the sentinel. Amara saw him pinch the sentinel's neck, and the giant fell unconscious to the walkway. Rabak bound him with the rope, ripped off part of the sentinel's sleeve, and used it as a gag to prevent him from calling for help when consciousness returned.

Amara rested a moment while Rabak carried Shadenni with him to explore their surroundings. He located an open window leading to an empty hallway and motioned to Amara to join him. He whispered softly, "We must search the halls until we find Watchful Ones guarding a door. That will be the king's chamber. We will conceal ourselves to await the coup. When it begins, we can try to save the king."

They tiptoed through the halls, down one passageway after another. Behind them Amara heard growls and turned to face the bared fangs of a vicious-looking guard dog. The dog eyed the intruders menacingly, but Rabak bent to one knee and whispered words in a language Amara could not recognize. The dog began wagging its tail. Rabak reached in his pocket and produced a small cake which the dog ate from his hand. Rabak caressed the dog as it lay down on the floor of the hall. Amara looked admiringly at her uncle, who whispered, "One needs many skills to be a successful thief. Someday I shall help you learn some of these skills."

They continued their search of the palace. Finally they turned a corner and saw Watchful Ones on duty before the king's door. Rabak and Amara jumped quickly back out of view, but not before one of the Watchful Ones noticed motion from the corner of his eye.

"Wait here," he told his companions.

He drew his sword and approached the corner to investigate. Rabak and Amara ducked quickly behind a curtain. The Watchful One rounded the corner and looked carefully in all directions.

"There's something moving behind a curtain," he called back. "Send me two more men."

Amara couldn't stop herself from trembling. The three Watchful Ones drew near. Just as the first one started to plunge his sword into the curtain, Shadenni squirmed in Amara's arms and jumped to the ground and out from behind the curtain. He meowed loudly and ran down the hallway. The Watchful One saw the cat and smiled at his partners.

"We are not the only ones keeping guard at midnight," he said. "Our royal master's palace will be kept free of rats."

They laughed and returned to their station in front of the king's bedchamber.

Cold sweat dripped from Amara's face. She held her breath until the guardians' footsteps receded around the corner.

Time passed as she and Rabak waited patiently in silence, peeking out occasionally from behind their curtain. In the distance, she heard the bell in the city's clock tower ring twice. As if from nowhere, armed men suddenly appeared, shouting and running toward the king's door. The Watchful Ones drew their swords and engaged the attackers. The attackers fought briefly, then fled, chased by the king's protectors. The air filled with smoke. Rabak grabbed Amara by the arm. "Now!" he said. They slipped through the smoke and into the king's chamber.

The room was filled with confusion as other groups of men rushed through the smoke in all directions. Amara lost track of Rabak. The smoke was too thick for her to see two men wrapping a motionless body in a carpet and spiriting it into the hallway. Finally the air cleared but Rabak was nowhere to be seen. Watchful Ones seized Amara. Across the room a man she had never seen before was also held captive by the Watchful Ones. The king rose from his bed.

"Well done, my faithful guardians. You shall be handsomely rewarded for repelling this traitorous attack." He paused, looked at the prisoners. "You may release the child. She appeared by magic to warn me of the plot. Take her to the palace gates and send her away." He looked directly at Amara. "Come to the palace on the morrow and bring your parents. I will reward you generously."

Amara had not had the chance to warn the king, but maybe she had had some small part in preventing his death. Certainly her family could use any reward he might give them. She bowed and let one of the king's guardians lead her out of the palace.

The king turned to the Watchful Ones. "As to the other prisoner, dispose of him in the manner prescribed for traitors to the realm."

Amara returned to her hut, awakened her parents, and told them the night's events. Rabak had not returned.

"I lost him in the smoke," said Amara. "I hope he didn't stay behind to take anything."

Her father nodded grimly. If Rabak had been tempted to steal some of the palace's treasures and was caught in the act, death was the best that he could hope for.

"When we see the king tomorrow, we can beg that my reward be freedom for Uncle Rabak," said Amara.

Her parents went back to bed and tried to sleep, but Amara was still too excited to relax. She left the hut and wandered to the river. As she approached the bank she could see a glow coming from beneath the water. The high, mysterious chorus of the watervoices echoed in the air.

High in the castle, chamber covered with smoke,
The kingdom lies saved, the plotters uncloaked.

Amara understood this part of the song, but the watervoices continued.

High in the castle, a tale of three kings,
Darkness can cover mysterious things,
One king has parted, another will leave,
The third will then reign, from the morrow's new eve.

Confused and exhausted, Amara returned to the hut and finally dropped into sleep.

*

Morning arrived, and Taran, Asuma, and Amara appeared at the palace gates as requested. The giant guards were reluctant to admit them, but orders from the king had to be obeyed. The three peasants were taken into the throne room.

Amara and her parents stood timidly at the door to the royal chamber. They had never seen such luxury, never even been able to imagine it. The brilliant light of crystal chandeliers reflected from marble floors and shimmering tapestries. The king, wearing magnificent robes, was seated on a golden throne. Haughty nobles stood silently around the sides of the room. The king summoned Amara's family forward. They approached the throne and bowed deeply.

The king spoke, "Before I reward this worthy family, there is another matter to be disposed of." He pointed to Maleviol.

"You, whom I have trusted and placed above all others in the realm, have broken my trust and committed high treason." He turned to his guardians. "Watchful Ones, loyal and worthy protectors of the throne, let us demonstrate to all present the fate of traitors."

Maleviol attempted to escape, but was surrounded quickly by Watchful Ones with drawn swords. The king stepped forward and extended his left arm, pointing directly at the prisoner. The First Minister raised his arms in defense and a look of terror flashed across his face. The king murmured words in an unknown language and a brilliant ray of light flashed from the tip of his index finger to the traitor, who disappeared into a misty cloud of smoke. When the smoke cleared, Amara saw, on the spot of ground where Maleviol had been standing, a large furry gray-and-white rat, whose beady eyes darted all directions in fright. Shadenni emerged from beneath the royal throne, and the courtiers laughed as he chased the rat from the hall.

The king turned to face the assembly and spoke to them.

"I now have an announcement of great importance. Those of you in this room have served me well for many years, and it has been my honor to be your king. I am now getting old and am without an heir. As my reward to Amara for having saved my life, I appoint her father Taran to be henceforth the new king of this realm. Taran, step forward."

Taran looked around in puzzlement as a buzz of anger arose from the assembled nobles. Then he raised his head high, straightened his shoulders, and approached the throne. The king removed the crown from his own head and placed it on the head of Taran. He continued to speak to the assembly. "Taran is now the crowned king of our nation. I have one last proclamation before I place him on the throne. Since the kingdom is now without a First Minister, I appoint to that office Taran's brother-in-law Rabak, formerly known as Rabak the thief, who will return from his travels in one week's time."

The nobles stood stunned in their places, expressions of resentment on their faces. But the king's commands were the law of the land. Applause, first hesitant then enthusiastic, greeted the new king as he took the throne.

He spoke quietly, with a great authority in his voice that Amara had never heard before, "Courtiers, I will be honored to serve as your king with all the powers I possess. Let us make ready for a royal banquet this evening to celebrate this occasion."

The nobles and palace courtiers responded to his tone of command and bustled out of the throne room to make their preparations for the banquet. Amara and her parents were left alone with the former king. Amara looked closely at him. His face was that of the king, but something about him seemed familiar. The mysterious words of the watervoices echoed inside her head.

> *One king has parted, another will leave,*
> *The third will then reign, from the morrow's new eve.*

She stammered, "Your majesty... I mean your former majesty... I mean..."

He smiled at her and winked, "Do you not recognize me, your uncle Rabak?"

Amara asked, "How… how… what… ?"

"My dear niece, by the time we had entered the king's chamber, the assassins had already murdered the king and it was too late to warn him. But I, Rabak, am the greatest thief in the world! During all the confusion and smoke, I stole the plotters' enchantment so that it would be I who would appear as the king and wield his mystic powers. When the enchantment ends in one week's time, I will again appear as your uncle Rabak, returning from his 'voyage.'"

*

Time passed in the realm, and the watervoices' song continued without end. Whenever the moon lay low in the sky and the glow came from within the water, the voices sang of the wise and prosperous reign to come of King Taran and his First Minister Rabak. They told of the gentleness of Queen Asuma and of the great beauty of Princess Amara. They also told of a cat, taken by the princess from the alleys of the city to live its days in the luxury of the royal palace.

Chronicle the Second
Princess Amara

Chapter One

Princess Amara felt rays of sunlight come through curtains on the high windows in her room. She yawned, stretched, and looked around her sleepily, trying to remember where she was. Finally she remembered that she was a princess and that she lived in the royal palace of the kingdom of Weltoria.

It was all very new to her.

For her whole life she had been a peasant girl, living and playing in the streets of the city and along the banks of the river. Her father had recently been crowned king of Weltoria, and Amara and her parents were newly installed residents of the palace. She had an entire bedchamber just for herself. Used to sleeping on straw in a corner of her parents' hut, she now slept on a soft down mattress covered with silk sheets.

She stretched and slid off the slippery sheets onto the richly carpeted floor. She pulled a cord which rang a bell, and a maid immediately appeared with a washbasin and cloth for Amara to wash her face and hands. Another maid helped her out of her nightgown and into her dress.

In the mornings she no longer ate with her parents. Instead, servants carrying silver trays brought breakfast to her bedchamber. She sat at a table to be served. A bowl of warm grain was placed in front of her, accompanied by fruit juice and milk. She poured cream from a silver pitcher over the cereal, and spooned sugar into the bowl. The next course consisted of cooked eggs with smoked meats, and she finished with a sweet roll filled with chopped nuts and dried fruits.

After breakfast in her previous life, she would have swept the mud floor of the hut when her parents had left to work in the fields. Today, she walked through the palace to the royal library, where she would join other children to learn the subjects necessary for those who would someday be rulers of the country.

Her feet were heavy as she walked down the stone floors of the dark and gloomy palace hallways. As the sound of her steps echoed from the arched ceilings, every echo seemed to tell her that she was an imposter, that she did not belong here. From the servants' quarters below came the aroma of cooking and the sounds of people at work. She would have loved to go downstairs and make friends, but servants were not permitted to be familiar with nobles. The ones she saw along her way bowed and stood quietly at the side of the hallway until she passed. When she came to the door of the library, she hesitated before entering. It would take strength to face what lay ahead of her.

Schoolwork was hard, and for the first time in her life she was glad that her parents had forced her to learn how to read. It had not been easy to stay indoors looking at her family's only book while all her friends were outdoors playing. But now, while she could not read as well as her classmates, she could make some sense out of her assigned work.

She had the best teachers in the kingdom to instruct her in the many subjects a royal princess must know. Her fellow students were sons and daughters of the highest nobles in the land. Even these were not admitted to her classes in magic and sorcery, in which she was the only student. These occult arts were permitted to be known only by the royal family itself and the royal magicians.

She forced herself to open the door and enter the library. The other students were already there, waiting for her. They gave her the same stony, resentful looks that they did every day. They knew she was really just a lowly peasant, and they did not let her forget it.

As the morning went on, Amara felt more and more out of place. The teachers seemed to miss no opportunity to make her feel stupid, although they covered their disdain with honeyed words – "Oh, is this too hard for the little princess? Let's have her try something a little easier" – while the other children suppressed their giggles. She thought the morning would never end, but finally the lessons were over.

Amara left the library with her head down and walked sadly along the palace corridor toward her chamber. Her steps were slow and echoed hollowly against the walls. Her shoulders were slumped and her head was down. She did not look at all like a happy princess. Entering her bedchamber, she threw herself on the bed, sobbing. All alone in the world, no friends with whom to spend time and play. This was not how being a princess was supposed to be.

Until a few weeks earlier she had been a normal girl with friends to play with every day. Her life had changed when her father and mother had suddenly been crowned king and queen. Amara now lived in a luxury that she had never even dreamed of. Her meals were the finest delicacies available in the realm. But she no longer had the freedom to run through the city and country that she had had before. A princess must be protected from her father's enemies, and all kings had enemies, men who could see themselves replacing the king on his throne. Even within the palace walls there were always plots underway, plots that might involve the kidnapping of the king and queen's only child, Princess Amara, heir to the throne.

Her father and mother spent all day, every day, learning the many things necessary to rule a kingdom. Sometimes they worked well into the night. Amara couldn't ask them to interrupt their duties just to spend time with her. She must rely on her own resources to learn how to cope with her new life.

Amara missed her friends from the city, and she had hoped to make new friends among the noble children in the palace. So far, this had not happened. The other children were polite to her, but only because they were required to be polite to a princess. They never invited her to do things with them or to visit them. She was all by herself. Her only friend in the palace was her cat, Shadenni, who had come with her from the streets of the city.

As Amara lay with her face in the pillows, she felt Shadenni jump onto the bed. Amara rolled onto her side and cuddled Shadenni, who started to purr. As Amara caressed the cat's head, she noticed a bleeding cut behind one ear. She looked closer and found other cuts and wounds. The little animal seemed to have been in a fight.

"Poor Shadenni," she said. "Whatever has happened to you?"

Life should be safe in the palace grounds for the cat, who no longer had to battle for survival in the streets of the city. There was nothing in the palace that could harm a cat.

Amara sat straight up in bed. Nothing *in* the palace? Shadenni must have some way of getting out of the palace, some way of getting to the freedom of the outside world. Amara wiped the tears from her eyes. If a cat could find a way out, so could a princess. She started forming a plan for the next day.

*

Early the next morning, Amara did not ring for her maids. She rose and poured water from a jug into her water basin, washed her face and hands, and dressed herself in her palace clothes. She pulled back the curtains and saw Shadenni sleeping in the court below. She hurried into the corridor and down the steps to the courtyard. When she arrived, Shadenni was arching his back and stretching in the first rays of the sun. He washed his legs with his tongue, stretched again, and entered the door that led to the kitchen area of the palace. Amara followed him. Shadenni trotted down a hallway that passed the kitchen and took a turning to the right. Amara had never been in this part of the palace before. Leaving the kitchen noises behind, she followed the cat to the end of the hall and down another stairway to the left.

At the bottom of the stairs was a doorway with its door standing ajar. It looked as though it had not been closed for years. Outside the door was a gutter that was open to the sky above, between high walls on both sides. Shadenni ran down the small stream of dirty water to where it entered an ancient drainpipe. He disappeared into the pipe. Amara walked carefully down to the pipe's entrance, holding her robes above the water. The pipe was dark and dingy, and curved out of her sight. As her eyes grew accustomed to the darkness, she could barely make out a glimmer of light down the pipe. This had to be Shadenni's secret way to the outside world. The pipe was just large enough for someone Amara's size to crawl through it on her elbows and knees. Pleased with her morning's discovery, she retraced her steps to the courtyard.

*

Through the rest of the morning and the early afternoon, she could scarcely contain her excitement. When school was over and the other noble children had gone, she hurried back to her chamber. Deep in the bottom of one of her chests covered by many fine robes and dresses lay the old ragged clothes she had worn before she became a princess. She quickly stripped off her finery and put on the peasant garment. She wrapped herself in a cloak and hurried downstairs, through the hallway past the kitchen, and out to the drainage ditch. Careful to keep the cloak from getting dirty or wet, she folded it and laid it on the top of the pipe. She slithered on her elbows and knees through the pipe toward the dim light at its other end. Popping her head out, she found herself in a fenced yard filled with refuse from the market that was held daily outside the walls of the palace. Her clothes were damp and muddy, and she smeared mud from them onto her face and into her hair. No one would ever connect this filthy, ragged urchin with the royal princess Amara. She slid open the gate to the yard, just a crack, and dashed into the busy market and freedom.

Shouts from vendors hawking their wares surrounded her. Smells of spices and food cooking on open fires were on all sides. It was wonderful to be back in the familiar world she was used to. A merchant, taking pity on the poor little girl who was looking so hungrily at his wares, gave Amara a skewer of partly burned chicken. She devoured it, licking every bit of grease from her dripping hands. It tasted better to her than all the finest foods served in the palace dining hall.

She was not able to stay outside the palace for long. Darkness came rapidly, and she needed to return before she was missed at the evening meal. It was the only time during the day that she could spend time with her parents and she couldn't be late. She hurried back through the pipe, wrapped herself in her cloak, and dashed back to her chamber to wash herself and change into fine garments for the evening banquet.

Night passed, and brought a weekend day with no school or lessons. Immediately after breakfast was over and the servants had gone, she put on her old clothes, wrapped herself in the cloak, and hurried to the drainage pipe. She crawled through the pipe as fast as she could and ran through the streets to her family's old hut.

When she came to the mud lane that led to the hut, she found her friends playing there. They looked at her with astonishment. Then they came forward slowly, shyly bowing, not seeming to know how to act toward a princess.

"It's just me, Amara," she said. "I've missed you so much, being stuck in that palace." She went among the children, ready to beg them to still be friends, when she felt a hard push in her back. She turned to see the cold blue eyes of a farm boy, Kasto, staring at her. His dark hair formed storm clouds around his face, which was set in stone. Just as her tears started to come, his eyes sparkled and his mouth broke into a wide smile.

"Bet you can't catch me," he teased, shaking his curly hair. Amara set off at full speed, chasing him, followed by the rest of the children.

The sun was low when Amara remembered that she had to be back at the palace. She waved goodbye to her friends and ran back to the drainpipe. She crawled quickly under the wall and returned to her room.

*

From then on, Amara would sneak out of the palace every weekend to play with her friends. Her spirits improved so much that
her life became better in all ways. Her schoolwork improved and
her teachers and classmates seemed to treat her with more respect. Her parents would worry if they knew she was leaving
the palace, but she felt sure no harm could come to her as long as
she was surrounded by her playmates.

Afternoons were the hardest part of every day. Amara
could not seem to make any progress in learning magic.

The Royal Magician towered over her. The stars covering
his robe flashed with intimidation, and his tall conical hat grew
threateningly taller. "You aren't even trying," he said, with a
trace of disgust in his voice. "Whisper the words *'objecto motiamus,'* and concentrate on the pencil."

Amara stared at the pencil sitting on the table in front of
her. Tears were glistening in her eyes. She had been trying for
over half an hour to get the pencil to move, even just a little. No
success at all.

"Object movius!" she screamed, but the pencil just sat
there, motionless.

"We'll try again tomorrow," sighed the magician. "It's not
like you need to learn difficult incantations. Simple spells for il-
lusions and healing are all a princess has to know. Your father
has already learned his magic."

Amara looked up with tears staining her eyes. "I can't do
it!" she said.

"You'll catch on one of these times," said the magician. "The secret is to concentrate your entire being on wanting to make the object move. I don't think you really care."

I do care! she thought. But deep inside, she realized it didn't really make any difference to her whether the pencil moved or not. She was going to be a failure as a princess. How could her father have changed so easily from being a poor farmhand into being the king? It seemed like he had been born to the throne. But she was still the same little peasant girl she'd always been.

Chapter Two

Amara let all her frustrations pour out of her on the next weekend when she escaped the palace to play with her friends. She had never run so fast, climbed such high trees, or swum farther in the river. Now she was challenging Kasto to see who could do the most dangerous and risky stunts.

"Dare you to go down-river," she taunted.

Down-river was a wide stretch where the river spread out, forming islands and dense stands of trees and undergrowth. Parents warned their children of the dangers that lurked there, in both human and animal forms. Kasto took the dare, and the two of them left the other children behind and plunged into the jungle. They swam across muddy swamps and pushed their way through thick stands of trees. Early afternoon found them lying on the riverbank, drying out in the sun, when Amara noticed Shadenni across a clearing. The cat seemed to be stalking something that was hidden in thick bushes under a grove of trees.

The cat was excited, with its tail sweeping rapidly back and forth, and its back steeply arched. It looked back toward Amara and Kasto, as if it wanted them to follow it.

"What's wrong with your cat?" asked Kasto.

"Let's find out," replied Amara.

They jumped up and followed Shadenni into the bushes. As they left the sun and entered the shadow of the jungle, the cat stopped. It lowered its head, with both ears flattened to the sides and its tail held rigidly straight back. As Amara and Kasto waited behind the cat, they heard the sound of a horse whinnying quietly in the woods ahead of them.

"Be careful," whispered Kasto. "My father said that bad people down here capture children and sell them for slaves."

The two children tiptoed as quietly as they could toward the sound of the horse. As they drew closer, they heard the sound of metal clanking on metal. Ahead of them was a clearing, and they could see several horses tied to trees on one side of it. On the other side was a large tent. Two men wearing helmets stood in front of it, with large swords sheathed on their belts.

"We'd better get out of here," whispered Kasto.

Amara was frightened, too, but she didn't like the idea of armed bandits roaming her father's kingdom.

"Let's sneak around to the other side of the tent and see if we can find out who they are," she whispered.

They crawled quietly through the undergrowth to the other side of the clearing and up to the back of the tent. There was a gap between the ground and the bottom of the tent, and they slid on their bellies up to the gap and peered up into the tent. Several heavily armed men stood inside. The eyes of their leader smouldered with hatred as he paced back and forth in front of the others.

"We move this afternoon," he said. "I've searched for years, and finally he's come out of hiding. They thought they could save him by sneaking him out of my kingdom, but my time has come. By the time the sun sets tonight, Taran will be food for vultures!"

Amara stared at Kasto.

"We've got to warn my father," she whispered.

The two children started to crawl away from the tent, but before they could move, they felt themselves grabbed by strong hands. The two watchmen had come quietly around the tent and trapped them. They were carried through the clearing to the tent door.

"Look what we found," announced one of the watchmen. "Two little spies. Shall we cut their throats and throw them in the river?"

The leader thought briefly.

"No," he said. "They'll make good slaves. Chain them to the tent post and we'll come back for them after we attend to Taran."

A man opened a chest and brought out locks and chains. The children were pushed roughly onto the ground.

"Let us go!" said Kasto, and struggled to get to his feet.

One of the guards struck him twice across the face with the chains, and Kasto sank quietly to the floor, blood oozing from cuts in his cheeks. The men sat the children back-to-back with the center tent pole between them. He wrapped a heavy chain tightly around their bodies, so tight that Amara could scarcely breathe. After locking the ends of the chain together with a large padlock, their captor tossed the key on a low table near the entrance to the tent.

"Take good care of the tent while we're gone," he snarled, with a nasty laugh.

The men pulled large capes out of a storage chest, and wrapped themselves so that their swords and armor would not show.

"We ride to the city," the leader said. "We'll leave our horses at the outskirts. Then we'll stay out of sight until dusk, when Taran takes his daily ride through the city. It'll be the last ride he ever takes!"

The men followed him out of the tent, and the children could hear them mounting their horses and leaving the camp. As soon as the sound of hoofbeats died in the distance, Amara struggled to get loose from her bonds.

"Are you all right?" she asked Kasto.

"I think so," he said. "Let's try to move this tent pole."

But it was too heavy for them to budge, and the chain was too tight for either of them to escape. It dug deep into their midsections, and every move they made seemed to make it dig even deeper. Amara thought about her father and mother back in the palace, not suspecting the coming ambush. She knew that she and Kasto would need a plan if they were going to be able to warn her father in time. Her mother's brother Rabak had been the best thief in the kingdom before he had been appointed First

Minister by Amara's father. What would he do if he were trapped like this? She thought and thought.

As her eyes wandered around her surroundings, she saw the key to the padlock lying on the table across the tent. What were those magic words the Royal Magician had been trying to teach her?

"I have a plan," she told Kasto. "It may not work, but one of my teachers told me that if I really wanted to make something move, I could use some magic words."

She stared at the key as hard as she could. *"Objectus motiamus,"* she whispered, straining to concentrate all her willpower on the key.

It remained motionless on the table.

"Objectus motiamus," she said louder, trying to visualize the key sliding across the table. Still nothing happened. The veins were standing out on her face as she became more and more frustrated.

"I can't do it," she sobbed.

"You can! You can!" said Kasto. "I know you can. Keep trying."

Amara took a deep breath. *"Objectus motiamus!"* she shouted as loud as she could, focusing all her anger on the stupid little key.

Her eyes widened as the key trembled in its place, then slowly, very slowly, began to slide across the table. As she concentrated harder and harder, the key started to move faster. She needed only to get it off the table and slide it across the tent floor to where she could pick it up and undo the padlock. The key slid to the edge of the table, and off – when it landed, it bounced twice and landed behind a large chest.

Amara struggled to make the key move again, but without being able to see it, she had nothing to focus her magic on. Tears of frustration and disappointment dripped down her cheeks. Behind her she could feel Kasto's shoulders droop. Then, out of the corner of her eyes she saw a small shadow appear at the tent door.

Shadenni appeared, looking at something behind the chest that was hiding the key. He moved silently across the tent floor and pounced out of sight behind the chest. Amara and Kasto could hear the sound of the cat playing behind the chest, batting something back and forth. Shadenni appeared from behind the chest, carrying a prize in his mouth. He walked proudly across the floor, his tail straight up in the air, and dropped the key in front of Amara.

Amara took no time at all to pick it up and open the padlock. She and Kasto threw off the chain, and Amara hugged Shadenni as tightly as she could. Then, letting the cat go free, she looked at Kasto. Blood dripped from the cuts in his cheeks, but he stood up straight with determination on his face.

"I'm all right," he said. "Let's warn your father."

*

It took the rest of the afternoon to get back to the city center. It seemed twice as long and hard to make their journey back as it had taken them to get out to the tent. Jungle bushes tore at Amara's clothes; mud in the swamps seemed to grab her legs and feet; river crossings were deeper and had stronger currents.

As they entered the outskirts of the city, Amara's legs started to give out. She couldn't slow down now! The two of them dashed through the city streets. When they ran past the food stands in the market, Amara felt her stomach protest that her last meal had been a long time ago. She ignored the pain and pressed on. Her lungs were bursting and ready to collapse when they finally reached the palace.

Evening shadows completely covered the palace walls. Inside the gates, Amara's father was getting ready for his ride through the city. The tired, dirty children ran for the entrance. Two palace guards blocked their path.

"You've got to let us in," cried Amara. "I'm Princess Amara, and I need to warn my father."

The guard chuckled. "Of course you're a princess," he said. "Let me help your royal highness."

He bowed low to her, then picked her up and tossed her as far as he could into the street in front of the palace.

"Don't let me see you around here again," he roared. "What kind of a fool do you think I am, to think a street urchin like you could be a princess."

She pulled herself back to her feet. In the courtyard behind the guards, Amara could see her father put his foot in the stirrup and mount his horse. Tears came to her eyes. Just as she was starting another attempt to get past the entrance, she heard Kasto whisper, "Watch what I'm going to do."

He moved to the opposite side of the gate. A horrible sound came from deep within him. She saw him writhing in agony, frothing at the mouth, and emitting blood-curdling

screams. Everyone stared at him, and the two guards ran to see how they could handle this new problem. As soon as their backs were turned, Amara flashed past them and into the courtyard. Her father, dressed in regal robes and wearing his crown, was mounted on his horse high above her. She grabbed at his leg. "Daddy, Daddy! Don't go riding. I have to warn you."
Taran looked at the mud-covered little girl in puzzlement. She wiped her face. "Daddy, it's me."

Taran recognized his daughter and jumped off his horse. "What's going on?" he asked.

Amara was beginning her story when the two guards rushed up holding the struggling Kasto.

"What is Kasto doing here?" asked Taran. "We'd better go inside and hear about this."

Amara told him everything that she and Kasto had seen and heard. As he listened, her father grew more and more serious. When she finished, he summoned a servant.

"Take these children to Queen Asuma and get them washed up. Find clean clothes for the boy and dress the wounds on his face." Taking Amara by the shoulders, he looked directly into her eyes. "I have business to take care of. When I return, there are many things to be explained."

As Amara and Kasto were taken into the interior of the palace, she heard her father calling for the entire force of Royal Guards to meet in the courtyard, prepared for battle.

*

Hours later, Amara and Kasto, clean and dressed in new clothes, were sitting with Queen Asuma when they heard the sounds of horses and soldiers returning to the palace courtyard.

Her father strode into the chamber.

"You can be proud of your day's work," he said. "Our kingdom is now safe from the invaders, and our neighbors in Laritia are freed from an oppressive ruler."

"But, but…" stammered Amara. "I don't understand."

Her father sat down. Her mother put her arm around Amara's shoulders and Kasto, his face wrapped in bandages, sat with Shadenni in his lap. Taran leaned forward in his seat, facing the children, and told them the story of how, years before, the king and queen of the neighboring kingdom of Laritia had been murdered by an evil prince, the king's nephew. The rightful heir to the throne was the king's only child, a little boy.

"That was me," her father said.

Faithful servants had smuggled Taran out of the palace and out of the kingdom before he too could be murdered. They had taken the boy to be raised by peasants in Weltoria. Taran and his adopted parents were the only ones who knew the secret.

"Didn't Mother know?" asked Amara.

"When your mother and I were married, I told her and her family," Taran went on. "We were content to live our lives as ordinary people. The most valuable things in life have nothing to do with wealth or power. We had good friends and a daughter we loved more than anything in the world. I worried about the people of my country, suffering under the rule of the murdering tyrant, but there was nothing I could do."

When Taran had become king of his new country, he could no longer hide from his old enemy. His cousin had sought him out to complete the gruesome task begun so many years before.

"Thanks to you two, not only is Weltoria safe, but I am now king of Laritia as well. From now on, the two kingdoms can become one, and live in peace."

*

Storytellers relate how the newly united kingdoms of Weltoria and Laritia prospered under the reign of King Taran. They also tell how Princess Amara was beloved by the people of both countries for her friendships with commoners as well as the nobility. And they tell how, despite the dangers that lay ahead for both of them, the special relation-ship grew between Princess Amara and her closest friend Kasto, the strong and handsome young soldier.

Chronicle the Third

Sword and Arrow

Chapter One

Amara struggled to stay on her feet. Her sword arm was growing tired and her opponent was pressing his advantage. The tip of his sword was getting closer to her chest with every thrust he made. Sweat dripped down her face, clouding her vision. She couldn't let it end this way. Perhaps she could make him overconfident, just for a second. She let her sword drop lower, pretending to be more exhausted than she actually was. Her adversary, seeing her "weakness," pulled back his sword and thrust it with what would be the killing blow. As his weight shifted forward, tipping him slightly off balance, Amara ducked low, knocked his blade aside, plunged her weapon directly at his exposed chest, and struck - nothing! He spun deftly to the side, letting her blade pass harmlessly by his side, and drove his own sword point directly into her rib cage, knocking her to the ground, flat on her back.

Kasto pulled the protective helmet from his head, loosening his flock of dark curly hair. The thin scars in his cheeks glowed red with exertion as he offered a hand to pull her back to her feet. Amara gritted her teeth as she accepted his help.

"I thought I had you this time," she said. "I guess I'll never catch up to you."

The two friends laid down the blunted training swords with their padded tips, and turned to the instructor for his evaluation.

"Well done, both of you," he said. "You may rest for a moment. I have a matter to discuss with you."

Amara dusted herself off and looked up at her friend. The scar lines on his face made him look older than his fourteen years. It seemed only yesterday that she and Kasto had been equals in size and strength. In the past two years, he had grown tall and muscular. Even though Amara herself was a fine warrior, the only weapon with which she could still beat him was the bow and arrow.

They seated themselves on benches at the side of the practice courtyard. The instructor spoke to Amara.

"Thus far, we have concentrated your training on skills you may need to defend yourself. It is not likely that you will ever go into battle with our army."

Amara didn't understand where this was heading.

"It may happen, however," he continued, "that you will need to assume command of parts of the army in time of war. You will need to learn military strategy and tactics to be a good commander."

She now began to understand what she was being told. Every kingdom had a school for future military commanders, the elite soldiers who would lead its troops in case of war. Most of the students were boys, but in Weltoria, Amara was the heir to the throne, the only child of King Taran and Queen Asuma. A future ruler must have the skills to protect herself from any dangers that might lurk in the shadows, men waiting for an opportune time to dispose of her and seize power. Amara had studied swordsmanship, archery, and other combat skills side-by-side with sons of the noble families of her kingdom.

The highest level of training, however, was in an international camp for young cadets from all of the Eight Kingdoms. It was held every two summers in the mountains of Thuringia. Could this be what their teacher was leading up to?

"Our future queen must have the best training available," he said. "You, Amara, will be one of our three representatives at the international academy this summer."

Amara felt honored to be chosen. She was worried about the other choices.

"Won't Kasto be going?" she asked. "He's the best cadet in everything."

King Taran believed that the high ranks of the kingdom should be enriched with talented additions from the ranks of commoners, so a few promising boys from non-noble families were invited to the training school. Kasto was one of these. His father was a successful farmer, but of common blood. Kasto was a life-long friend of Amara, and he had built himself into the finest fighter in the school.

The instructor smiled. "Of course Kasto will be going," he said. "There can be no question of that."

"We are honored," said Amara. "Who else have you chosen?"

"Another easy decision," said the instructor. "Simontor is also highly skilled. He surpasses everyone except Kasto with the staff, and is close to you two at swordsmanship and archery. The three of you will represent our kingdom with honor."

Simontor was indeed an excellent choice. He was the heir to one of the most noble and distinguished families in Weltoria. A small, wiry boy, he seemed to have been born handling a staff. The staff was a six-foot-long rod of wood. Both its side and its ends could inflict punishment, and Amara's ribs bore painful bruises from training sessions against Simontor. He was an aggressive fighter, and, like the other boys in the school, he made no concessions when in combat with Amara.

"When do we leave for the academy?" asked Kasto.

"Not for a month," said the instructor. "We shall spend that time preparing you for the conditions you'll face. At the academy you will be trained for the rigors of warfare as well as in higher levels of the combat skills you've been working on here. This will not be a holiday, it'll be the most demanding challenge you have ever faced."

Amara and Kasto looked at each other and saw the determination in each other's eyes. Whatever the elite academy had to offer, they would be ready for it.

*

One month later, Amara, Kasto, and Simontor rode into sight of the camp where the academy was to be held. From a hilltop, they looked down on a broad river valley. Tendrils of smoke trailed upwards from campfires set among peaked tents. The camp was located next to the river. Across the valley, cliffs of white granite formed a wall at the opposite side of the valley floor. High mountains, snow-capped even in summer, loomed behind the tops of the cliffs.

Amara and her friends had traveled far across Weltoria and halfway into Thuringia. An entourage of her father's soldiers had accompanied them to the border, and a Thuringian escort had been with them the rest of the journey. Although Amara knew how to change into peasant garb and blend in with the common people, while traveling as an official representative of the kingdom she and the two boys needed protection from possible attacks by enemies of her father.

Twenty-four young cadets would be attending the academy, three from each of the Eight Kingdoms. Because Amara's father was the king of two countries, three of the students would be from Laritia, his other kingdom. Amara was curious to meet the boys who would be coming from her father's true homeland, the land of his birth.

Most of the journey had been across plains and through farmlands and pastures, but this day had brought them into wilder country. They had been surrounded by dense forests, and Amara's eagerness to reach the academy had grown steadily as they rode over hills and through canyons. Mountains that had once seemed distant on the horizon towered above them as they rode into camp. After days of summer heat in the flatlands, the tired travelers took deep breaths of cool mountain air and slid off their horses. They lifted their bags from the packhorses and looked around. The academy's staff had already raised tents and the camp was filled with boys milling about, looking for the ones they had been assigned to. Amara, Kasto, and Simontor eyed the scene of confusion. A staff member approached Amara.

"Your tent is over there," he told her, pointing to a tent nestled under a stand of leafy trees a short distance from the main camp. "You girls will have some privacy from the other cadets."

Girls! So there would be at least one other girl. Amara left the two boys and carried her bags toward her tent. As Amara approached the tent, a tall dark girl, wearing the green and silver uniform of Laritia, waited for her in front of it.

"My name is Zismelda," she said. "I am honored to be sharing a tent with my Princess Amara of Weltoria."

Was there a note of mockery in her voice? Amara could not decide. She smiled at Zismelda.

"I am delighted to meet you," she replied. "But let us leave the 'Princess' behind us. At this academy we must all be equals, and I suspect that we two girls must be more equal than the others."

They looked back at the center of the camp, where boys were strutting back and forth, trying to look calm and dignified while flexing muscles and stretching to their tallest height at the same time. The girls smiled at each other and Zismelda seemed to relax.

"Equals we shall be," she said. "You are fortunate, though, to have such a tall, good-looking traveling companion. We do not have boys like that in our part of your father's realm."

Amara said nothing in reply, and began moving her gear into the tent. Zismelda had arranged her sleeping blankets and other equipment neatly on one side of the tent, and Amara laid out hers on the other side. A large tree branch over the tent provided welcome shade from the late afternoon sun. Amara lay down on her blanket and looked up at Zismelda.

"When do we report?" she asked.

"When the sun gets low we are to go to the evening meal," answered Zismelda. "After the meal, they will tell us tomorrow's schedule."

She stopped abruptly and stared at one of Amara's bags.

"Your bag just moved," she said.

Amara picked up the bag and shook out its contents. Along with various items of clothing, a large cat fell to the ground. It looked around and stretched, then went up to Amara and rubbed against her legs, purring loudly.

"Shadenni, what are you doing here?" asked Amara. She turned to Zismelda. "My cat traveled with me to the border. The soldiers were supposed to take him back to the palace when they returned. He must have escaped."

Zismelda seemed to be trying to control herself, but couldn't suppress her laughter.

"Please don't tell anyone," begged Amara. "If the boys found out I brought a cat, I'd be humiliated." She paused in thought. "He doesn't like to be away from me. Sometimes it seems almost that he keeps guard over me."

Zismelda promised to keep the secret, and the two girls rested from their travels until dinnertime.

*

A clanging sound aroused them, summoning the cadets to their meal. Amara walked through the twilight toward the small village of tents that formed the main camp. Campfire smoke and the smell of roasting meat welcomed her to dinner. Pushing her way through the crowd of boys, she was able to find Kasto and Simontor. As they waited in line to get their food, she asked them if they were in the same tent.

"They separate kids from the same country," Kasto said. "They want us to live with boys from foreign lands. I think it's supposed to help prevent wars in the future if we understand each other better."

"Maybe," said Amara skeptically. During her father's few years as king, she had learned that sometimes the greatest danger could come from those who were most trusted.

"I've already made a good friend in my tent," said Kasto. "He's from Druria and his name is Limlan. We both wanted the same spot for our sleeping rolls, so we wrestled for it."

Boys are strange, thought Amara. "You became friends even though you beat him in wrestling and took his sleeping place?" she asked.

Kasto grimaced. "I didn't actually beat him," he said. "He was stronger, and I wasn't quick enough to keep him from putting me down." He smiled at Amara. "It was a good time," he added. "We're going to wrestle again tomorrow just for fun."

They picked up metal plates, onto which the cook dropped huge slabs of roasted meat and large slabs of flat bread. Finding an open spot of ground not far from the main campfire, they sat down to eat. Amara pulled out her dagger, a large knife with a sharp point and foot-long blade, and sliced the meat into smaller pieces. She tore off a piece of bread, wrapped it around a hunk of meat, and began eating hungrily.

"Whatever comes tomorrow, at least they're feeding us well tonight," she said, as meat juices rolled down her chin.

Kasto and Simontor were eating with equal enthusiasm, and the surrounding noise grew quiet as everyone in the camp concentrated on their dinner. Amara was wiping the last bit of gravy from her dish when a tall man with a gray beard approached her group. The three students jumped to their feet and bowed deeply. This was the academy's director, Gongzu, making his rounds to greet each delegate individually.

"I am pleased to welcome you three to our academy," he said. "Amara's father is well-known to me. I trust that we can expect the highest level of performance from his daughter and her companions."

"We are honored to be here," replied Amara, as humbly as she could. "I promise that we will all give the greatest effort of which we are capable."

"During the next days you will find that you are capable of much greater effort than you now suspect," said Gongzu. "Enjoy the rest of the evening – on the morrow you shall begin your work."

They bowed again as Gongzu departed. Sundown had brought a chilling mountain breeze. It didn't feel like summer here in the foothills. Clouds overhead blocked the moon and stars, and thunder sounded not far in the distance. Amara had difficulty keeping her eyes open as waves of fatigue from the journey washed over her. She said goodnight to the boys and trudged slowly back to her tent. As she pulled back the flap to enter it, she felt a few drops of rain land on her shoulders. She looked up gratefully at the large tree branch that sheltered the tent. If a storm came up during the night, she would have at least some protection.

Sleep came as soon as she had rolled herself up in her blankets. She was vaguely conscious of Zismelda coming into the tent, but she fell quickly back to sleep.

Chapter Two

In the middle of the night something sharp scratched Amara's cheek and she woke up abruptly. Shadenni was standing at her face, meowing loudly. Amara could barely see the darkened outline of the cat as it faced the tent entrance, arched its back, and hissed loudly. She felt the blankets next to her, but Zismelda was gone. Rain fell heavily outside. She crawled to the tent opening to find out what was upsetting Shadenni. She and the cat had no sooner poked their heads outside than she heard a huge crash and felt the tent collapse behind her. *What was going on?* In the blackness of the night she couldn't tell what had happened. Then a flash of lightning showed something that froze her in place. The large sheltering branch, almost a foot thick, had come off the tree and fallen on the tent. If she had stayed in her blankets, she would have been crushed to death.

Amara quickly took stock of the situation. She reached back into the collapsed tent and pulled out a cloak to cover herself against the rain. It was fortunate that Zismelda was safe, that she hadn't been in the tent. But where was Zismelda? No sooner had the question come to Amara than she felt Zismelda touch her shoulder.

"What happened?" asked Zismelda. "I needed to relieve myself and went into the woods. I heard a crash."

Amara was shaking as she told her about the branch falling on their tent. Just as she finished, two guards from the main camp arrived, carrying torches.

"I thought something had happened over here," said one of them. "With all the wind and rain, we weren't sure if we'd heard anything."

The guards helped the girls rescue their sleeping gear from the tent and took them to a larger tent in the main camp. Its floor was mostly covered with sleeping boys, but there was enough space for the two girls to put down their blankets. Amara lay as quietly as she could, but adrenalin was pumping too hard for her to fall asleep. Her life had been saved by Shadenni. Zismelda had been lucky, too. Finally, Amara drifted into a troubled sleep that lasted until dawn.

*

Breakfast came early the next morning. Amara rose, went to the river and splashed water on her face, and walked to the food tent. Kasto was waiting for her, standing next to a tall, well-built boy with brown eyes and long brown hair.

"This is my friend Limlan," he said, and stopped as he saw Amara's face. "What's the matter?" he asked. "You look like you haven't slept."

Amara told him about the night's events.

"You're lucky to be alive," said Kasto.

Simontor joined them for breakfast and Amara repeated her story to him. Before the day's activities started, the three Weltorians left Limlan and walked through the frigid morning air to retrieve her belongings. Altogether they had just enough strength to drag the branch off the tent. While Amara crawled into the collapsed tent to assemble her gear, Kasto examined the branch carefully.

"Look at this," he said.

Amara and Simontor looked where Kasto was pointing, at the end of the branch that had pulled loose from the tree. Instead of a rough, broken surface, part of the end of the branch was smooth, with only a small amount rough.

"Most of this branch was sawed through," Kasto said. "It looks like a recent cut."

The three friends stared in silence. Simontor was the first to speak.

"Someone must have climbed the tree during the storm last night," he said. "The noise of the wind and rain kept you from hearing them cutting the branch loose."

"That's what upset Shadenni," said Amara. "He must have sensed someone up there."

"They were trying to kill you and Zismelda," said Kasto. "You two have enemies in the camp."

"Zismelda wasn't in the tent," started Amara, then broke off. "She said she had gone out for a moment. Either the assassin didn't see her leave, or... "

The unspoken words hung over them. *Or else she was the assassin.*

"From now on, we have to watch her closely and keep an eye on you as well," said Simontor. "Shouldn't we report this to Gongzu?"

"We don't have any proof that she was the one," said Amara. "I'll be on my guard to see if she tries again. If she does, I'll be ready for her."

*

The morning went smoothly. The subject was swordsmanship, and Amara found she was able to hold her own against the boys from other countries. Some of them made the mistake of beginning their duels with her hesitantly, as if they were uncertain of how to fight against a girl. The first few jabs of Amara's padded sword tip into their ribs taught them that it would take all the skill and strength they possessed just to defend themselves.

At morning's end, Amara was tired but pleased with her efforts and ready for lunch. Zismelda joined her.

"Thanks for moving the tree off our tent," said Zismelda. "I've got all my stuff moved into our new tent." She told Amara that they now had a new tent, located in center of camp, close to the main campfire. "This is much better," she went on. "Instead of keeping us away from the boys, now we'll be surrounded by them." She smiled with satisfaction. "Speaking of boys, that good-looking boy from your kingdom – Kasto, I think his name is – has been watching me this morning. I think he likes me."

Amara felt a twinge of something. It couldn't be jealousy, she didn't think of Kasto in that way. She pulled herself together. This could be good. If Zismelda thought that Kasto was interested in her, she wouldn't be suspicious of him keeping an eye on her.

"Maybe he does," said Amara. "I'll see what I can find out and tell you what he's thinking."

*

The afternoon subject was archery. Amara was excited to have the chance to show off her best skill. She left the tent carrying her familiar bow and a quiver of arrows. In the distance she saw a row of targets, farther away than any she had ever shot at. The cadets groaned as they lined up, facing the targets.

The instructor for archery was Gongzu himself. "In battle," he said, "you need to be able to hit your enemy before he can hit you. The well-trained soldier must practice accuracy by shooting at long-range targets."

Amara squinted at the distant target. She drew an arrow and fitted it to her bowstring. She calculated in her head. Not much wind. The target slightly higher than where she was standing. She drew her bow as far as she could, aimed carefully, and released the arrow. The arrow followed its path and hit just inside the edge of the bull's-eye. Her next shot was better, hitting well inside the bull's-eye, and the remaining three shots stayed on target. It had taken all of Amara's strength just to get her arrows to reach the distant targets, but her shooting was as accurate as ever.

Up and down the line of cadets, sweat dripped from young faces as they strained to hit the distant targets. One other target had three arrows in the bulls-eye and two in the next closest ring. Amara looked down the line and saw that it was the target in front of Zismelda. None of the other cadets was as accurate, but they had all placed their arrows somewhere into their targets. This was indeed an elite group of young warriors.

Gongzu called for their attention. He looked pleased. "Very good," he told them. "You seem to be well-trained at the basics."

The basics? thought Amara. *How could the hardest shooting she had ever done be only the basics?* She soon found out.

"Your enemies in combat will not be as cooperative as those targets," said Gongzu. "They will not remain still so as to be easily hit. Rather, they will be making every effort to take evasive action. You will now begin your training in hitting opponents who are moving."

The cadets were given ponchos of heavy cloth to protect the front of their bodies down to the knees. They received masks that covered their faces, with slits to see and breathe through. Finally, a packet of ten arrows was placed into each quiver.

"These arrows have clay tips," said Gongzu. "They will fly as accurately as ordinary arrows, but they won't penetrate your ponchos or masks."

The cadets were divided into two groups and placed on opposite sides of a large field. Amara looked around and saw Kasto standing near her. Simontor and Zismelda had been assigned to the other side. Gongzu instructed the cadets to keep moving so as to evade the other group's arrows, standing still just long enough to aim and shoot at their opponents. Amara rushed her first two shots and missed them badly. She took a longer time to aim her third arrow, and was rewarded by seeing it hit the chest of a cadet on the other team. She waited too long to move on, though, and felt an arrow from the other side hit her poncho. This was complicated!

Her next three shots found their targets, however, and she kept moving well enough to avoid being hit again. She was aiming her seventh shot when something crashed into her from the side, knocking her to the ground. As she fell, she saw a bright object flash past her head. Around her, she heard instructors shouting to cease combat. A heavy weight was pressing her to the ground. It moved off her and spoke.

"Look at the arrow that just missed you," said Kasto, pointing several yards behind them.

Amara's eyes followed his. The arrow that was sticking in the ground didn't look like one of the ones they had been using. Kasto stood up and retrieved it.

"I saw its metal point flash when she took it out of her quiver," he said. "She shot it so fast that I only had time to knock you out of the way."

Amara looked at the arrow. Its flight feathers were green and silver. She looked up to see Zismelda pushing through the circle of cadets and instructors that surrounded her.

Zismelda took the arrow from Kasto. "I didn't see the arrow until I released it," she said. "It must have gotten mixed in with the training arrows somehow." She was shaking and looked like she was about to cry.

Gongzu stepped into the circle. "Don't feel responsible," he said. "You couldn't have seen the difference in the arrows at the same time you were running and taking aim." He looked round the circle. "It is difficult to know how this mistake could have happened. Perhaps one of my instructors has been careless. I must apologize on behalf of the academy to Amara, and also to Zismelda. War games are dangerous. Our staff will redouble our efforts to ensure that no further accidents can occur."

The cadets were dismissed for the rest of the afternoon. As they and the instructors left the field, Zismelda remained behind with Amara, Kasto, and Simontor, who had joined them.

"I feel so guilty," she said. "I should have been more careful. I should have checked all my arrows."

"Don't worry about it," said Amara. "Accidents can happen."

Zismelda left the three friends and hurried back to camp. As soon as she was out of hearing, Kasto grabbed Amara's arm.

"Do you think it was really an accident?" he asked.

"No," said Amara. "But I don't want to make her suspicious. I have to sleep in the same tent with her every night. Gongzu thinks it was an accident. I can't accuse her without more evidence."

"I have important news," said Simontor. "I was talking to the other cadets from Laritia. Did you know Zismelda is your cousin?"

Amara shook her head. "What do you mean?" she asked.

"Her father's brother was the king of Laritia. He was killed trying to assassinate your father."

"Then that means..." Amara hesitated, thinking. "That means if I should die, her father would be heir to the throne."

The three friends were silent for a moment. Kasto broke the silence.

"So that's her reason," he said. "I think we should tell Gongzu."

"We don't have any proof," said Amara. "If I accuse her, Gongzu would need evidence. Without it, he might send both of us back home. I don't plan to let her cheat me out of this training." She thought for a moment, and turned to Kasto. "She thinks you like her. Try to encourage her. If you spend every spare minute with her, she won't have time to plan anything else against me."

"I'd rather spend time with a snake," said Kasto. But he was willing to do whatever it took to protect Amara, and he reluctantly agreed to the plan. "Don't you have any magic spells to protect you?"

"I've only learned how to use magic on things I can see," answered Amara. "And magic can't read people's minds. There's no way to use it to find out what she's planning to do next. It's up to you to find out everything she is planning."

*

The plan seemed to work. Amara went the next few days without any attacks. She kept herself on guard at all times. Strangely enough, the only times she felt truly at ease were when she was alone with Zismelda in their tent. She knew that Zismelda would not dare attack her when she was sure to be found guilty.

Amara's worst moments came when the boys discovered Shadenni living in her tent. They taunted her unmercifully until she was rescued by the camp's cook. Mice and other small forest animals were attracted by the supplies in the food tent, the cook told them. Each morning Shadenni presented his trophies from the previous night's hunting. The cook explained very clearly that unless the boys wished to have their meals prepared with vermin-infested food, they should show appreciation to the cat and his owner.

Along with training in physical combat, the cadets also received instruction in military strategy, tactics, and map-reading. At lunch on the seventh day of the academy, Gongzu announced the next day's project. At breakfast, the cadets would be divided into three-person teams. Each team would be given a map describing a route for them to follow. Each team's route would be different, and take them through territory they had never seen before.

"Your routes will be difficult, even dangerous, and they will challenge your strength and endurance. For this reason, you may have this afternoon and evening to rest yourselves."

Amara had never heard such welcome words. After days filled with vigorous, stressful combat training, her body was bruised, tired, and aching. She returned to her tent immediately after lunch and collapsed on her sleeping blankets. She lay dead to the world until she was roused by the bell that signaled dinner. As she pushed herself groggily to her feet, she realized that Zismelda was not in the tent. Her sleeping blankets were still rolled up, just as she had left them before breakfast.

Amara found Kasto with his friend Limlan in the line waiting for dinner.

"Did you see her this afternoon?" she asked.

"No, she disappeared after lunch. I though she'd gone back to your tent."

"She wasn't there," said Amara.

They were joined by a sweaty, out-of-breath Simontor.

"Have you seen her?" he gasped.

"We haven't seen her since lunch," said Amara.

"I saw her leaving camp, so I tried to follow her," he said. "I lost sight of her. I've spent the whole afternoon trying to pick up her trail, but I couldn't find her."

They got their dinner plates and sat down to eat in silence. Halfway through the meal, they were joined by Zismelda.

"I almost missed dinner," she said. "It was too noisy here in camp, so I climbed up the cliff to get some peace and quiet. I lay down on a flat rock and fell asleep."

Silence greeted her, broken by Amara.

"I'm glad you finally got here," she said. "You need a good meal tonight to be ready for tomorrow."

As they were cleaning the last bits of food from their plates, an instructor handed each of them a small piece of paper.

"These are your team members," he said. "Get together with them at breakfast tomorrow."

Amara looked at her paper, and her heart sank. She was teamed with Zismelda, along with a boy whose name she didn't recognize. Zismelda was smiling.

"This is wonderful!" she said. "The two of us will be together. And with that handsome boy from Bauria! We'll have a great time!"

Spending the day hiking with Zismelda through dangerous mountain terrain was just what Amara did not want to do.
She didn't seem to have any choice.

"Bedtime for me," she said. "Tomorrow morning is going
to be here soon."

She said goodnight to Simontor and Zismelda. Kasto
walked with her part of the way, as she trudged slowly back to
her tent.

"What can I do to guard myself?" she asked.

"Don't ever let her get behind you. I'll see if I can think of a
better plan tonight." He patted her shoulder and headed back to
the campfire.

Chapter Three

The next morning when Amara and Zismelda went to breakfast, they were joined, not by the boy from Bauria, but by Kasto instead.

"He said he didn't want to go on a dangerous hike with two weakling girls," he said. "I was happy to trade with him." He gave Zismelda a big smile. "I like hiking with girls."

Zismelda looked like a lioness whose prey was within her grasp. "And I like boys who like to hike with girls," she said, eyeing Kasto hungrily. "This will be a great day!"

After breakfast they went to the cooking tent to pick up their food for the day. The girls returned to their tent to prepare their packs, and were joined shortly by Kasto. They split the food among their three packs, and each of them took a canteen full of water. They would be hiking fully armed, with dagger, sword, bow and arrows, and staff.

Amara arranged her pack on her back and stood up to test it. The load was heavy on her already-tired body, but not too heavy for her to carry. She was grateful for the month they had spent conditioning themselves before coming to the academy.

She had just laid her pack back down when Simontor appeared, carrying two maps.

"They gave me your map when I picked up the one for my group," he said, handing one of the maps to Zismelda. "See you tonight."

Zismelda glanced briefly at the map. "We'll start out going up the valley," she said, and tucked it teasingly into her pouch.

"We'd better see the map, too," said Kasto. "We all need to learn how to use maps."

Zismelda took the map back out of her pouch and held it in front of her. "Get as close as you can," she said. "We can all look at it at the same time."

Amara and Kasto each stood on one side of her. Zismelda held the map toward Amara, so Kasto would have to press against her to see it.

"I like this," she said, wiggling against Kasto. "We should read maps together more often."

The map was crudely drawn, just as they had been warned.

"In battle, maps are drawn hastily, with whatever materials are at hand," Gongzu had told them. "The maps you'll be using will be of that kind."

Just as Zismelda had said, their route began by taking them up the valley. They would come to a fork in the river, at which point it seemed that they would climb up a ridge. To go on from there, they would need to locate landmarks that were marked on the map.

As they stood up, Shadenni came from the interior of the tent and rubbed against Amara's leg.

"He wants to go with us," she said. She tucked the cat into the top of her pack, his head just peeking out.

Zismelda handed the map to Amara. "As princess, you must be the leader. If you have trouble following the map, I will be able to help. My father has taken me hunting many times in mountains like these."

"I should have no trouble finding our route," said Amara stiffly. "I also have been hunting with my father."

They hoisted their packs and began their journey. As they set off, she worried about having Zismelda behind her. Over her shoulder she saw Kasto following next in line. As long as he stayed between her and Zismelda, she would be safe. She heard Zismelda talking in a low voice to Kasto and giggling. Amara gritted her teeth and pressed forward.

It took a good hour to get to the river fork. The hikers took off their packs and sat down to have a short break. Amara munched on some hard cheese and bread, washing it down with cold water from her canteen. Shadenni hopped out of her pack and disappeared into the undergrowth next to the trail. When it was time to shoulder their packs and begin the steep climb out of the valley, he had not returned.

"Shadenni usually knows what he's doing," said Amara. "He'll catch up to us when he feels like it."

The rest of the morning was spent climbing into and out of steeper and steeper canyons, as their route took them high into the mountains. Sometimes the trail skirted the edge of cliffs where one misstep could plunge them down to jagged rocks hundreds of feet below. Amara didn't feel comfortable not being able to see Zismelda behind her. Hopefully Kasto could keep her distracted until they got to safer terrain.

When they broke for lunch, the mountaintops seemed almost close enough to touch. Far below them lay the river valley they had started out from. The air was cold and refreshing to the sweaty hikers. They unshouldered their packs, unbuckled their swords, and lay down their bows and arrows. The three of them examined the map.

"We must be at the half-way point," said Zismelda. "The route seems to be turning back toward camp."

Even though they lingered almost an hour over their break, it still felt too short. Amara wearily put her weapons back on and hoisted her pack. She unfolded the map and began the next stage of their hike.

Half an hour later, she was leading them along a section of trail less than two feet wide that clung to the side of a canyon wall. She edged slowly along the path, placing one foot in front of the other with great care. The trail was rocky, with dead leaves from the trees above covering parts of it. As she rounded a bend in the cliff, she heard a rustling of leaves above her and Shadenni slid down the cliff and landed on the trail. He stood stiffly before Amara, arching his back and hissing loudly. She raised her hand to signal the others to stop.

"What's happening?" asked Kasto, whose view of the path ahead was blocked by Amara.

"Shadenni's back," answered Amara. "He doesn't like something about the trail ahead of us."

She used her staff to poke at the leaves and rocks on the trail. It seemed to be firm and solid. She poked harder, and rocks ahead of her started to move. With a roar, the path vanished into a rockslide that clattered into the canyon below them. Where the path had been, there was now nothing but empty space. Two more steps along the trail, and Amara would have been lying crushed at the bottom of the canyon.

Her whole body was shaking as she backed away from the slide and down the path behind her. She felt Kasto guiding her until she reached a section of trail wide enough to turn around. Legs still rubbery, she followed him until the trail widened and turned into a small valley. The three of them took off their packs and sat down. Shadenni jumped into Amara's lap. His presence comforted her as she stroked his fur. Once again he had saved her life.

"Something must be wrong with our map," said Kasto. "I know the instructors checked out all of the routes before they gave out the maps."

"We have to go back the way we came," said Zismelda. "It's mostly downhill. We can get back to the river before dark, and from there the trail is easy. I'll lead."

The tired cadets put on their packs. Shadenni disappeared into the brush again as they set off down the trail back to camp.

It was more than two hours after dark when they finally got back. They were immediately summoned to see Gongzu.

"We were about to send out a search party," he said. "What has happened?"

Kasto told the story of the rockslide. Zismelda gave the map to Gongzu. He looked at it briefly.

"This is not one of our maps," he said. "Where did you get it?"

"Simontor picked it up for us when he got the one for his group," said Kasto. "I guess it was in the same place where all the maps were picked up."

He hesitated, and looked at Amara. She shook her head. Gongzu had a grave expression on his face.

"Someone must have substituted it for your map while the other cadets were picking up theirs," he said. "This is very serious. A second incident threatening Amara's life. This one is clearly not an accident. I shall place a watch on Amara. Nothing will happen to you at this academy. Be sure never to be out of sight of your guards except when you're in your tent."

Amara and Kasto found Simontor and walked to the food tent to see if they could locate some leftover dinner.

"Zismelda must have switched maps," said Kasto. "Remember how she stuck the map in her pouch as soon as she had it. When we asked to see it, she pulled out the fake map."

"She admitted she was familiar with country like this," added Amara. "That's where she was yesterday afternoon! Without a heavy pack and weapons, she easily had time to explore the mountains until she found a washed-out place on a trail. She drew out the false map and had it ready to use." She thought for a minute. "And that's why she wanted me to be the leader."

"We've got to get evidence," said Simontor. "I'll ask my friends in camp to look for anything they can find that would help us."

The cook had saved dinner for them. After finishing it, they all went back to their tents for the night.

Chapter Four

The next day went smoothly. Kasto stuck close to Zismelda, and Amara could tell that there was always at least one staff member within sight. She was able to concentrate on the day's training activities.

That evening, the academy instructors had a treat planned for the cadets. After dinner, everyone was to gather around the campfire for the instructors to put on a show of the most advanced techniques and skills that they knew. These were the finest warriors in the eight kingdoms, and the cadets were excited to be able to see them in action.

Dinner had just ended when Kasto came running up to Amara. "I've lost her," he said. "She went running into the darkness heading upriver, but by the time I tried to follow she'd disappeared. You'd better go back to your tent and lie low."

Amara hated to miss the show, but standing in the light of the campfire she would make an easy target for an arrow coming out of the dark woods. Kasto walked back to her tent and offered to stand guard.

"I'll be safe enough in here," Amara said. "I've got my sword close by, and I'll keep a hand on my dagger. Zismelda is a good fighter, but she wouldn't have a chance against me in fair combat. You don't need to miss the show."

Kasto reluctantly agreed to go back to the campfire.

"I'll check back here every now and then," he said as he left. "Please let me do that, just so I won't worry."

Amara lay down on her blankets, keeping the dagger in her hand. As she looked up, she saw a shadow move across the tent. Frightened, she rolled onto her front and slid her head out of the tent opening. Dagger in hand, she looked up – and saw Kasto standing guard.

"You scared me!" she said. "Please, go watch the show. I can protect myself."

She watched him out of sight as he went back to the demonstration. She lay back again and tried to relax her body while keeping her mind alert. The boys' cheers rang out from the campfire area. Amara was angry that she couldn't be there. She couldn't decide if she hated Zismelda more for trying to kill her or for making her miss the show.

Outside the tent, a light suddenly flared. She looked out her tent flap to see Limlan. In one hand he carried a torch and in his other hand was a piece of paper.

"A message for you," he said.

Amara took the paper and read it in the torchlight. It was from Simontor.

I have the evidence we need, it said. *Meet me right away in the first clearing downriver. Hurry!*

Amara tucked her dagger into its sheath and ran for the trail down-river. As she left the camp the trail plunged into darkness. She hesitated before entering the forest. She had forgotten to bring her sword. Should she go back for it? The first clearing wouldn't be far, and Simontor would be there if she needed any help. She plunged into the woods.

The moon had come up, and there was enough light coming through the trees for her to see where she was going. Before long she could see the moonlight in the clearing ahead of her.

She paused to look out into the clearing for Simontor. The clearing was empty. Was this a trap? Just as she realized she had been deceived, she felt a heavy blow on her neck that knocked her to the ground. A second blow, from a staff, she thought, came crashing down, but she escaped most of its force by rolling to her side. Zismelda must have circled around the camp to lie in wait for her.

Somehow she found out that we suspected her, Amara thought. *The note was a forgery.*

A blow from the end of the staff caught her in the ribs. She rolled herself off the trail and into the woods. The trees were thick enough that Zismelda could no longer swing the staff. Amara looked up to try to see her adversary. In the dim light she could barely see a shadowy figure wearing a hooded cloak. It covered her opponent's head and body, and made her almost invisible. She poked at Amara with the end of her staff, but Amara saw it coming and rolled behind a tree. *If I could just get to my feet!*

A sliver of moonlight showed Zismelda tossing the staff aside and drawing her sword. She came forward, stabbing it down toward Amara's heart. Amara rolled away, caught a low branch with one arm, and pulled herself to her feet.

Why couldn't I have taken half a minute and brought my sword before coming out here? she thought.

Her opponent struck again with the sword. Amara lifted her left arm to ward off the blow, while pulling her dagger from its sheath with her right hand. Pain shot through her body as the sword sliced into her protecting arm.

Using the dagger, she deflected the next two strokes of the sword. Her eyes were getting used to the dim light among the trees, but her opponent's would be also. She felt herself getting weaker. She was losing blood and wouldn't be able to defend herself much longer. She needed a plan.

Maybe the old trick would work against Zismelda, the one she'd tried against Kasto. She let her right arm sink low, as if she were too tired to keep it raised. Her opponent took the bait and drove the sword straight for Amara's heart. She spun quickly to the side and used all her strength to drive her dagger toward her adversary's body. The hooded figure wasn't agile enough to twist aside, as Kasto had done. Amara felt her sword arm stiffen as her blade struck the shadow's chest and plunged into its body. She released the sword and jumped backward. A gurgling sound came from under the hood as her enemy collapsed to the ground with a groan and lay still at her feet.

Amara stepped back with horror, looking at the hilt of her dagger protruding from her fallen adversary's ribs. Along the trail behind her she heard shouting. She turned and saw torches coming toward her. Soon Kasto came into view, followed by Limlan. They ran to Amara as soon as they saw her.

"Limlan told me about the note," said Kasto. "We followed you…"

He broke off when he saw the blood covering her. She lifted her right arm and pointed to the ground in front of her. Limlan moved his torch to illuminate the fallen figure. Bending over, Kasto pulled the hood from its head. Amara gasped. The face was not that of Zismelda. It was Simontor.

His eyes opened and he focused on Amara with a look of pure hatred. His mouth opened, as if to speak, but nothing emerged but bubbles of blood. His eyes rolled back into their sockets, his head drooped limply to one side, and there was complete silence.

Kasto ripped a strip of cloth from Simontor's cloak and tied it around Amara's arm to stem the flow of blood while Limlan ran back to camp. He returned with a group of instructors. They carried Amara to the tent that served as an infirmary for sick and injured cadets. The deep cut in her arm was washed, covered with healing herbs, and wrapped in clean cloth. A final wrapping was wound tightly around all the dressings, so that no blood could escape, and the tourniquet was removed. She was given a potion of special herbs to help ease her pain and help her sleep. A team of instructors was assigned to watch over her throughout the night. Kasto would not leave her side, and Shadenni entered the tent and curled up at her feet.

She tried to sleep, but the excitement of battle had worn off and the pain in her arm was intense. Gradually, the pain-killing herbs took effect and she fell into an uneasy sleep.

A sound awakened her. She looked around the tent. The flickering candlelight showed her that Kasto and her guards were gone. A gush of cold air blew the tent flap open and Simontor limped into the tent. Blood was dripping from the hole in his chest. He raised his arm and pointed his finger at Amara.

"Murderer!" he groaned. "You must die."

Amara was frozen to the ground. She couldn't even raise her arms. Simontor came closer and closer, his blood dripping onto her body. He slowly raised his sword overhead with both hands.

Amara tried to shout for help, but only a croaking whisper escaped her lips. Before she could react, Simontor plunged his dagger down, straight toward her heart. She screamed and screamed.

Another sound entered her consciousness. "Wake up! Wake up!"

She blinked her eyes in puzzlement. Kasto was kneeling at one side and her other guardians at the other.

"It's all right," one of them said. "Just a dream. You were having a nightmare. We're here to keep you safe."

They gave her another bowl of sleeping potion, and before long she was asleep again. The night was the worst of her life. She woke up several more times from nightmares. In the morning she was unable to go to breakfast with Kasto and Limlan, so food was brought to her. She tried to eat, but the food was flavorless and she couldn't swallow it.

"I need to go home," she told her guardian. "I don't want to handle swords or other weapons ever again."

"Rest here this morning," was the answer. "Gongzu will meet with you after the midday meal."

Chapter Five

Her midday meal was brought to her, but again she was unable to eat. The sun had just passed its highest point when Gongzu entered the tent.

"Come with me," he said. He led her out of the camp. She felt dizzy when she first rose to her feet, but her muscles loosened as they climbed a steep trail over rocks and boulders. Gonzu stopped when they reached a summit that looked out over the river valley. Mountains rose behind them, and in the distance before them they could see the flat plains and farmlands of Thuringia.

"The lands we see, and your father's kingdoms beyond them, are filled with people: farmers, merchants, craftsmen," said Gongzu. "They need wise rulers so that they can live their lives in prosperity. But they also need strong rulers, to protect them against invasions from without and lawlessness from within."

Amara looked at his face, lined with the wisdom of experience. She could feel the warmth of the afternoon sun flowing into her body.

Gonzu continued, "A ruler's life is never easy. Those who are destined to rule cannot lead the lives of ordinary people. They must make decisions and perform deeds that can tear their souls apart. This is their duty, their responsibility to the people of their lands."

He turned his eyes from the horizon to burn directly into Amara's. "Last night you, Amara, had to perform the most difficult deed of all, taking the life of another human being. What you did was necessary, necessary for two reasons. First, because you needed to save your own life. Your first duty is to yourself. And second, to protect your kingdom. Simontor's father, Namintor, died after assassinating the king who ruled before your father. His survivors still covet the throne.

"A king without an heir becomes a target for those with ambitions to rule, and if Simontor had succeeded in causing your death, your father himself would have been in the gravest danger. You have prevented your kingdom from being taken over by a family of evil-doers."

Amara sat in silence, looking into the distance and listening to the words of Gongzu.

"You will never again be the innocent girl you were before yesterday. You have learned the true use of the weapons of war with which you cadets have been practicing. Your soul itself is wounded, but as that wound heals it will give you strength and wisdom. That strength and wisdom will help you grow to become the strong and wise ruler that your people will need."

He stood up. "I leave you here for the afternoon. Let the peace of this beautiful place enter into your heart. We shall expect you at the evening meal."

As he left, Shadenni appeared from behind a boulder. Amara took him into her lap. They sat quietly as the sun descended into the west and disappeared under the horizon.

*

The evening meal had already begun when Amara got back to camp. She got her food and found Kasto and Limlan sitting next to Zismelda, laughing and joking. Zismelda was so focused on Kasto that she did not see Amara arrive. Kasto jumped to his feet and made a place for her to sit between him and Limlan.

She settled herself on the ground and looked at Zismelda. "It seems that you were not the enemy after all. I will have to learn to trust you again."

"He was very clever in throwing suspicion on me," answered Zismelda. "I had told him I wanted to beat you in archery. It was important for me to impress my future queen with my abilities. Simontor knew I would be shooting mostly in your direction, so he must have sneaked the sharp arrow back into my quiver while I was listening to the instructors."

Amara reached across to Zismelda. "I am sorry that I suspected you of being the enemy," she said.

"I was sure that he was the one that was trying to kill you, but if I told you what I suspected, I thought it would just make me look more guilty," said Zismelda. "I knew his family had a hunting estate in these mountains, and he was the one who brought us the faked map. He must have known where the washed-out place on the trail was."

"He was gone all afternoon before we left, pretending to look for you," said Kasto. "It would have been easy for him to cover the gap with leaves and stones."

Zismelda nodded. "Last night he told me to meet him half a mile upriver. I had to go to find out what he was planning. Of course he wasn't there, and by the time I got back to camp, it was all over."

Tears came to Amara's eyes. She felt Kasto put his arm around her shoulders.

"We're your friends," he said. "I shall be at your side as long as I live. Zismelda, too. She and her father will always be loyal to you and your father, whatever the future may bring."

"I will also be your ally," said Limlan. "If you should ever journey to Druria, you can rely on me to give you any support you might need."

They ate dinner in silence, Amara feeling safe and secure in the company of her friends. Afterwards, they walked together to the girls' tent. The boys said goodnight, and the two girls entered the tent. The healing herbs were doing their work, and the pain in Amara's arm had almost disappeared. She was soon fast asleep. Shadenni curled up next to Amara. His warmth and purring helped her sleep soundly, and by the next day she was ready to go back to her training.

*

Amara completed the remaining two weeks of the academy with success. Her training in magic had taught her how to cast healing spells. Her wounded arm stayed in a sling for only a week, and before long her combat skills were as good as ever. She could feel a difference in the way the other cadets looked at her dagger. They knew that it had taken the life of her enemy.

She was the only one of them to have killed an opponent in combat. She didn't like the way it set her apart from the others, but this would be her life from now on. She would need to accustom herself to it.

Finally the academy was over. At breakfast the next morning they gathered one last time. One of the instructors rose to speak to them.

"It is the custom at each of these academies to recognize the most outstanding cadets," he said. "I have two awards to present."

The cadets listened with excitement. To receive an award at this academy would insure the recipients a rapid rise in the armies of their home countries.

"The first award is for excellence in all forms of physical combat," the instructor continued, raising a decorated scroll. "This award goes to Kasto of Weltoria."

The cadets applauded as Kasto rose shyly to his feet and received his scroll. When he had returned to his place, the instructor spoke again.

"For overall excellence in all phases of military science, the outstanding cadet at this summer's institute has been chosen to be Namla of Holunland."

Even louder applause surrounded Namla, one of the most popular boys at the academy, as he accepted his award. After he was seated, Gongzu rose and faced the cadets.

"You are different now from the people you were when you arrived. You have learned the highest skills in warfare that our instructors can teach you. You must remember that knowledge brings responsibility. Never shrink from using what you have learned, in defense of your kings and your countries, when it is necessary. But use every avenue possible to avoid the use of force."

His eyes ranged over the audience of cadets, touching on each one in turn.

"At this academy you have formed friendships and loyalties to cadets from other lands. I encourage you to continue those ties. Visit each other's kingdoms whenever possible, and maintain the bonds between your families.

"Go with my blessings. May your journeys be safe and your lives be prosperous and peaceful."

The cadets returned to their tents to finish their packing and load their horses. Limlan joined Amara and Kasto to make his farewells. Leaving him, they walked to see Zismelda. Exchanging embraces, they agreed to visit each other as soon as possible.

"When you come, don't forget to bring Kasto," said Zismelda to Amara. "Your father was wise to choose such a strong and brave companion to train with you," she added, flashing her eyes at Kasto.

Before long, all the cadets had mounted their horses and were headed back to their own lands. Shadenni was riding in a special basket on the back of one of the packhorses. As Amara rode along, next to Kasto, she looked across at him, riding straight and tall in the saddle. Under his shock of unruly black hair, his blue eyes reflected the sky. The scars in his cheeks gave his face an air of dignity. Why had she never noticed how good-looking he had become?

As if sensing her eyes on him, he turned his head and spoke. "One good thing about our suspicions of your cousin was that I got to spend so much time with her. She's very pretty, don't you think?"

Amara didn't know how to answer. She tried to stay calm. "Yes, she is," she said in a strangled voice.

Kasto looked puzzled. "Not as pretty as you," he said. "There's never been any girl in my life except you, and there never will be."

As he smiled at her, she felt a warm glow come through her being. Without her noticing it, her feelings about him had deepened. He was still her best friend, but he had become more than just a friend. This summer had changed her life in more ways than one.

Chronicle the Fourth
Kasto in Holunland

Chapter One

"It is time we dealt with this situation," said King Taran. "Nothing can be gained by further delay."

The king looked gravely at his two most intimate advisors. He had summoned his brother-in-law, First Minister Rabak, to meet with him and Queen Asuma to discuss a delicate situation that faced the royal family of Weltoria.

"Amara is now seventeen," Taran continued. "It is already very late to make arrangements for her marriage. Almost all the eligible princes in the Eight Kingdoms have already been claimed. We will need to look for younger princes, boys of fourteen or fifteen, to find an appropriate match for our daughter."

"That is not, in itself, a disadvantage," said Rabak. "When Amara becomes queen, she will be the ruler. A younger husband might be less likely to challenge her rule."

"True," said Queen Asuma. "But, of course, finding eligible princes is not the main problem we face."

The three sighed and looked at each other. The main problem that faced them was that Princess Amara might not wish to marry any prince at all. For most of her life, her closest friend had been Kasto, a commoner. Kasto was now an able and talented young man, a junior officer in the king's army, and Amara had eyes only for the warm smile and dark hair of her strong and handsome friend.

The only times he and Amara could meet openly were the training sessions when Amara practiced swordsmanship and archery. As the future ruler of her country, it was important for her to be able to protect herself against any possible attacks, so she had three practice sessions every week, working with Kasto under their instructor's supervision. These were their only official meetings, but the palace was a large complex of buildings, with many secluded spots where a young couple might happen to find occasional brief moments to spend together.

Rabak looked at the king and queen. "I have given this matter much thought, and I believe I have found a solution," he said. "I have made discreet inquiries of the First Minister of Holunland. It seems that it is possible to arrange for Kasto to spend a year there, as a page in the retinue of Lord Damier, the king's cousin. It may be that a year of separation will permit Amara's attentions to wander elsewhere."

"Very good," said Queen Amara. "And if the affection that Amara and Kasto feel for each other does not cool, the training he will receive as a page should prepare him for the possibility of being the Prince Consort to a future queen."

It was the custom for the sons of royal and high noble families to spend a year serving as pages in the courts of other kingdoms. Serving as a page gave a young man the chance to observe at first hand the ways that governing was done, the agreements and negotiations that kings must make with other kings and with powerful families in their own kingdoms. It was also an occasion to attend banquets and balls, to learn the social graces practiced by those of the highest ranks. Because a page would socialize with young ladies of nobility, it was almost unthinkable that a commoner could ever receive such an appointment.

"How were you able to get Holunland to agree to accept Kasto?" asked Taran.

"I spoke in the greatest confidence with the First Minister," said Rabak. "He and the king remember with gratitude the occasions that you, and in earlier times your father, have helped them to repel invaders from their eastern border. They privately understand that Kasto is of common birth, but they will let it be publicly known that he comes from a noble family."

Kasto's father was, of course, a commoner, but was an exceptionally able farmer. Beginning with a small plot of land when his son was still a small boy, he had built his farm into one of the largest in the land. He was, in fact, a very rich man. In recognition of his ability, King Taran had appointed him to serve as

Weltoria's Minister of Farming, and to oversee the royal farms as well as his own.

"We shouldn't expect Kasto to tell untruths," Rabak continued. "He can refer to his father as the Royal Minister, and that is certainly true."

"It is delicate, but I think it can work," said Taran. "There is yet another possible advantage to us. There is an excellent chance that he may someday rise to become commander of our army, and his training as a page will aid him greatly to meet the social and diplomatic demands he will face in that position."

*

The subject of this discussion was at that moment lying in pain on his bed of straw in the junior officers' quarters. His muscles were cramped and his head felt as though all the troops of the king's army were marching through it. A new sharp pain pierced his side. He looked up to see Rontes, a fellow officer, kicking him in the ribs.

"Get up, you lazy oaf," said Rontes. "Our morning of freedom is already half over, and you still lie abed."

Kasto groaned and pulled his cloak over his head. "Go without me. I'll never be able to move again."

"We need you to come with us. You were our entertainment in the tavern last night, and we must repay you with sweetmeats at the market today."

"I'll never take strong drink again," moaned Kasto. "Now I know why my father warned me against it."

Kasto's father did not permit the drinking of liquor in his house. Kasto had lived at home almost all his life, but he had recently left the farm to move into quarters with the other junior officers. Once a week, on the eve of their morning of freedom from duties, the young men spent the evening in one of the city's taverns. Until the night before, Kasto had contented himself with drinking spring water when he went to the tavern with his friends.

"Last night you thought that strong drink was wonderful," said Rontes. "We tried to keep you from taking too much, but you insisted in downing bowl after bowl of it. Now you are paying the price, but you must still come with us."

"Never," said Kasto, rolling face down on his mat.

"We think you will come," said another fellow officer. The two young men pulled off Kasto's tunic and leggings and grabbed him by the arms and legs. They carried their naked burden squirming into the stable yard, where they dumped him into the cold water of the horse trough. Kasto struggled to get out, but his friends pushed his head under again and again.

Finally, the cold soaking brought him into full consciousness. He relaxed, and his laughing friends let him climb out of the trough. Rontes wrapped Kasto's cloak around him, and he returned to the sleeping area to dry off and get dressed.

Minutes later, he reappeared in the stable yard.

"To the market," he said. "I'll eat enough sweetmeats to break your purses."

As the friends joined arms and headed for the market, a messenger blocked their way.

"Kasto is summoned to the royal presence," he told them. "Be at the entrance to the royal audience hall in one half of an hour."

The messenger turned and strode off.

Kasto looked at his friends. "What did I do last night?" he asked. "Have I brought dishonor to the royal army? Will I be dismissed from service?" His bright future was vanishing before his eyes.

"Discipline of junior officers is hardly the concern of the king," said Rontes. "Whatever may await you, it will have nothing to do with your misadventures last night in the tavern. It seems we will not have the pleasure of your company at the market, but at least our purses will remain full."

Kasto looked sadly at his companions leaving for their morning of fun at the market, and turned his steps toward the supply room. He slid out of the usual uniform that he wore every day, and put on the dress uniform that he and the other soldiers wore only for special occasions such as parades before important visitors. Whatever lay in store for him, he must present the finest possible appearance when summoned to see the king.

He could feel stares from the common soldiers as he left the military compound. His cheeks burned as he passed servants and nobles going about their business in the palace grounds. Why had he been singled out for a special appearance before royalty?

He arrived at the gates of the throne room fully ten minutes before he was due. Time seemed to crawl as he waited his turn to be called into the royal presence. The large wooden doors were carved with pictures of festivals and battles, hundreds of tiny people going about their duties. Kasto thought he had counted every one of them several times before he finally heard his name being called.

He was surprised when he entered the royal audience chamber. Instead of the usual clusters of nobles and dignitaries gathered throughout the hall, it was empty except for the king, the queen, and the First Minister. Kasto approached the throne and bowed deeply.

"At your service, my lord," he said, keeping his head bowed.

"Rise, Kasto," said Taran. "You have long been a friend of our family, so we may speak without undue formality."

"Yes, my lord," said Kasto, straightening up and lifting his head. Hopefully, whatever his punishment might be, for whatever crime, it would be tempered by the king's mercy.

"You have had a promising career in our service," began Taran. "You ranked first among the cadets in our military academy."

"Yes, sir," said Kasto. *Please don't soften the blow, just let me know the worst as soon as possible,* he thought.

"And, your superiors report that you also rank first among the junior officers," continued Taran. "Of course, in your time as an officer there has fortunately been no occasion to prove yourself in battle."

"No sir," said Kasto. *Where is all this leading?*

"It appears to us that your future will bring you to hold high ranks in our army, those ranks normally held only by nobles." Taran looked at his queen and at Rabak, then returned his gaze to Kasto. "In council, we have determined that you have been lacking in the opportunity to meet and associate with members of the highest classes." He paused. "Other than, perhaps, with our daughter."

"Yes, sir… I mean no, sir," stumbled Kasto.

"At any rate," said Taran, "we have decided that your career would benefit from a training period which would improve your skills in dealing with members of the aristocracy. Go now with our First Minister, who will explain what lies ahead for you."

He signaled that the audience was at an end. Rabak stepped forward, took Kasto by the arm, and led him out of the royal hall through a side entrance.

Kasto's thoughts whirled within him. *I'm not being punished! I think I'm being rewarded.* He followed Rabak down a corridor and into a small, dark side room.

"Be seated," said Rabak, indicating a low bench in the center of the room. Kasto sat down on the bench and looked up at Rabak.

"The king has determined that you should serve one year as a page in the household of a royal duke of Holunland," said Rabak. "It is a rare opportunity to observe at first hand the use of power at the highest levels. You will also move in the highest social circles."

Kasto looked up at Rabak, speechless. How could he, born a peasant, ever expect to associate with the nobility, let alone with royalty?

Rabak clasped his hands behind his back and walked around Kasto, observing him carefully from all angles. He continued, "There are also dangers. You will be a representative of our kingdom. Before we can send you we must be as certain as possible that you will do nothing that would bring disgrace on King Taran."

"I understand, sir," said Kasto.

"I do not think that you do fully understand," said Rabak. "But we will make sure that you do before you leave on your journey."

"How long will I have to prepare, sir?" asked Kasto.

"You leave in two weeks," answered Rabak. "Lord Damier expects you to assume your duties in his household three weeks from today."

Kasto's spirits dropped. "Sir, I don't see how I could learn so many things so quickly. I don't think anyone could."

"You forget, my boy, that King Taran, Queen Asuma, and I had to assume our places in the nobility with no training at all. I can assure you that, though difficult, it is possible. In two full weeks, twenty-four hours per day, we will have you ready. We start immediately."

*

It was not, in truth, a twenty-four hour per day training program, but every waking hour was used thoroughly. Kasto was drilled in all aspects of life as a noble. He learned the proper clothes to wear for each occasion, and how to wear them. He learned how to eat at a banquet table, when to use a fork, when to use a knife, and when to use both. He learned the proper phrases to use when addressing ladies and gentleman. Although Holunland spoke the same language as Weltoria, there were certain expressions that were different, and it was important not to tell a lady that you wanted to eat her dog when you wished to tell her that you hoped she was feeling well.

"It's too much!" said Kasto, trying for the fourth time to master the correct way of bowing to a Holunian duke as distinct from the way of bowing to a Holunian general. "I give up! I just want to go back to my father's farm."

Rabak was a harsh taskmaster. He brought a birch rod down smartly on Kasto's shoulders. "Losing one's temper is not possible for a page," he said. "Whatever is done or said to you, you must respond politely and respectfully. Now, show me the correct way to bow to a noble lady."

Kasto pulled himself together. He stood as politely and respectfully as he could and bowed deeply.

Dancing presented more difficulties. Kasto was a well-coordinated athlete, and was expert and enthusiastic in the farm and peasant dances he had grown up with. But court dancing was very different. Every gesture had to be delicate and refined, even when moving across a dance floor at full speed. He had hoped to practice dancing with Amara, but when he arrived at the palace ballroom for his first lesson, he found a palace matron waiting for him.

"I am Mullesvia," she said. "I have heard of you from my niece, Zismelda, in Laritia." She looked him over from head to foot and smiled with approval. "I see her description was no exaggeration."

Mullesvia was an excellent dancer, but every turn around the dance floor saw Kasto crunching her toes with his large feet.

"One-two-three, one-two-three," she chanted. "Spin-two-three, dip-two-three. Now you're starting to learn." She held Kasto in her firm grip as they twirled across the empty floor of the palace ballroom.

"Noblemen and noblewomen exchange polite phrases and witty remarks while dancing," she went on. "In your case, it might be best if you contented yourself with giving your partners a nice smile. Your pretty face and curly hair may distract your partners from noticing your lack of wit."

I must always respond politely and respectfully, thought Kasto. "Yes, your ladyship," he said.

Chapter Two

The two weeks were over before Kasto knew it. He was amazed by the amount of knowledge and new skills he had acquired, but was painfully aware of the long gap that remained before he could feel comfortable in the company of nobility.

"The purpose of your pageship is for you to grow into feeling at ease in the highest circles," said Rabak. "The only true teacher will be time, and you will find things easier every day as the year goes on. I look forward to seeing a polished and competent young man in a year's time."

That evening, Kasto walked through the shadows of the palace grounds and ducked into a small garden. Amara was waiting behind a large bush. They embraced.

"I wish you were not going," said Amara. "I suspect they are trying to keep us from seeing each other."

"Nothing can change my feelings for you," said Kasto. "I will miss you every hour I am gone."

He looked into her deep brown eyes. This would be the longest time they had ever been separated. He was already beginning to feel the pain of separation. "Your face will always be in front of me," he continued.

They kissed each other and embraced in silence. Finally Amara broke the silence.

"I wish you a safe journey," she said. "When you cross the river and leave Weltoria, part of me will go with you."

"This will be the longest year of my life," said Kasto. "I shall count the days until I can return to you."

*

Early the next morning, Kasto saddled his riding horse and loaded two pack horses with his necessities: Page garments for every occasion, military garments and uniforms, weapons, and the accompanying necessities of shoes, gloves, cloaks, hats, undergarments, etc. Kasto would make his journey with a traveling companion, who would see him safely delivered to the court of Holunland, then return to Balarta alone. Kasto had chosen Rontes to travel with him.

The two young officers rode out from the palace on a sunny spring day, with cool winds blowing the dust from their horses' hooves high into the air behind them. They crossed the wooden bridge over the river, which flowed peacefully under them. Wild ducks and geese flew past and landed splashing in the water.

"A beautiful day for a journey," said Rontes. "We finally get to travel together."

"I've been waiting for three years," said Kasto. "You should have been chosen to go to the academy with Amara and me instead of the traitor Simontor."

"Better late than never," said Rontes. "Just two weeks ago we were throwing your stupid body into the water trough," he continued. "Now you're off to join the big noses. I hope you'll not have forgotten us lowly junior officers when you return," he added with a smile.

"One year from now, if I'm lucky enough to survive my full period of pageship, I'll be back in quarters, sleeping on straw," said Kasto. "I hope you will not forget your long-lost companion."

Both the young men laughed and looked ahead of them, as they rode down the dusty road to the south.

*

It was a three-day journey to the Thuringian border, then another day across a corner of Thuringia to approach Holunland. All travelers were stopped at the Holunland border and required to explain their purpose for entering the country. When the turn of Kasto and Rontes finally arrived, the captain of the border guards examined their papers, which bore the royal seal of King Taran.

"You are expected, sir," said the captain. "Lord Damier's entourage awaits your arrival in two days." The border guards parted ranks to allow Kasto, Rontes, and their pack horses to pass into Holunland.

As the travelers rode on into the country, they noticed that a contingent of soldiers was stationed in every town along the way and even in some of the smaller villages. At the inn where they spent their first night in Holunland, Kasto asked the landlord about this.

"Well, young sir," answered the landlord, "we never know when the barbarians from the east will send a raiding party into our land. It was only two years in the past that this very town was attacked. Fields were burned and our livestock was killed or driven away. Three of our children were taken into slavery."

He was rewarded by looks of surprise from Kasto and Rontes.

"Our eastern border has no mountains to protect us from invaders," he explained. "Our king's army stands alert now to provide us the protection we need."

The Eight Kingdoms were bordered on the west by the ocean. To the north, east, and south rose high ranges of mountains that provided a natural fortress to protect the kingdoms from outside invaders. Kasto remembered having studied maps that showed a gap in this ring of mountains, a gap along the eastern frontier of Holunland that was filled only by a range of low hills. These hills were a wild and lonely place, with only a few small villages spread among dark forests and dangerous swamps.

"The eastern border is too long for us to build a wall," continued the innkeeper. "And also too long to be guarded at all times and places by our king's army. So the border is patrolled by soldiers, but our villages and cities need guardians also, for the barbarians are sometimes able to evade the border troops and ride deep into our country for raids."

"We are grateful for the protection given by your king's army," said Kasto. "We prefer not to be attacked by barbarians as we make our journey across your land."

The inn was a primitive place, but the hungry young men found the food excellent. They plowed into an evening meal of roast duck, potatoes and yellow squash. Large pitchers of ale were on the table, but Kasto drank only enough to quench his thirst.

"You seem to have learned your lesson well," teased Rontes. "I won't have to douse you in the horse trough tomorrow morning."

Kasto grimaced. "You don't need to remind me," he said. "That was a morning my head will never forget."

Their accommodation consisted of a small room in the rear of the building, next to the stables. The straw on the floor was fresh and deep, and they enjoyed a night of sound sleep.

*

The travelers rose early the next morning and ate a hearty breakfast of chicken soup, whole-meal bread, and eggs. Before long they were packed and riding along the highway. As the sun rose higher, the day grew warm.

At midday, they crossed a bridge over a rushing river. Kasto looked upriver to see the stream flowing out of a small woods.

"Let's have our meal in the shade of those trees," he suggested.

They rode along the water into the woods until they came to a small clearing next to a pond. A waterfall poured into the upstream side of the pond.

"Time for a swim," said Rontes.

They stripped off their sweaty clothes and jumped into the water – and screamed.

"This water is freezing!" shouted Kasto, after he had caught his breath.

The pond was shallow enough that the water came up only to just above their knees. Rontes waded over to the waterfall and let the frigid water splash onto his head and shoulders. As he looked up to see the top of the falls, Kasto tackled him and pushed him under water. They wrestled until Rontes was finally able to get his head above the surface and catch his breath.

"My revenge for my ducking in the trough," growled Kasto. "I've been waiting for the chance to settle my account." He pushed Rontes underwater again.

Rontes came up, gasping and laughing. "I'll grant you your revenge," he said. "Now let's have our meal."

The young men stretched out on the grass beside the pond and let the sun dry them as they ate their bread and cheese. They were reluctant to leave the peace of the woods, but eventually they dressed and resumed their hot journey.

After one more night in a village inn and one more morning's travel, Kasto and Rontes saw in the distance the skyline of a city that could only be Holunbar, capital of Holunland. As they drew closer, they began to make out the outlines of gigantic walls and towers. Their own capital city, Balarta, had no walls at all, its edges simply opened into fields and pastures. The only fortifications in Balarta were around the royal palace complex itself. Here, everything was different. The entire city was fortified. A large moat encircled the city walls.

Kasto and Rontes rode up to a group of soldiers who were guarding a bridge across the moat. They dismounted and Kasto showed his letter bearing King Taran's seal to one of the soldiers.

"I am here to join the household of Lord Damier," he said. "Please direct me to his palace."

The soldier spoke briefly to his captain, then returned to Kasto and Rontes.

"I shall show you the way, sir," he said.

Rontes took Kasto by the arm.

"It is time for me to return to Weltoria," he said. "I will travel much faster without the packhorses to delay me. There is enough daylight left to get a good start on my journey."

Kasto and Rontes clasped hands and embraced. Rontes remounted and rode back down the highway. Kasto watched him pass out of sight, looked up at the huge gates leading into Holunbar, and felt very alone.

"I will follow you," he said to his guide.

The soldier took the reins of one of Kasto's packhorses and crossed the bridge into the city. Kasto led his riding horse and the second packhorse and followed.

Once past the city walls, Kasto found that Holunbar was much like Balarta. Small houses and huts lined the streets just inside the walls. These gave way to more substantial houses as they passed further into the city. Outdoor markets appeared whenever more than two streets came together to form a plaza. Kasto smelled familiar scents of cooking foods, and heard familiar sounds of merchants bargaining and hawking their wares. Perhaps Holunland was not going to be as different as he had feared.

His guide led him to a gate in the middle of a long wall. He rang a bell, which was immediately answered by a man in uniform. Kasto showed the man his letter. The man led Kasto and his horses into a large courtyard. Kasto thanked his guide, who then left the courtyard and turned back in the direction of the city gate.

"I will summon the head of Lord Damier's staff," said the uniformed man. "He will show you where you will be living and explain your duties."

Kasto waited in the courtyard. The walls that surrounded him were of light-colored stone, with arches outlining doorways and gates on the ground level as well as windows on the higher levels. Through open gates he could see other courtyards with people walking busily through them, carrying out the daily activities of an active palace. In a while, a tall man entered the courtyard.

" I am Bardloro," said the tall man. "Follow me to the stables. You can unpack your horses and leave them there. I will then show you to the pages' quarters."

From the stables, Kasto was led through several courtyards to a gate.

"Your sleeping quarters are through the gate, first doorway to the right. You may carry your packs to your room and then rest from your journey. I will send for you later, when you shall be instructed in your duties."

Kasto thanked Bardloro and walked back to the stableyard to get his packs. He hoisted two of them over his shoulders and carried them to the door to his quarters. He pushed the door open. It was dark inside. He took his packs into the room. Before his eyes could adjust to the dark, he was tackled and thrown to the floor by an invisible opponent. His opponent pummeled him about his head and shoulders. Kasto struggled, but his opponent was stronger and pinned his body to the floor.

"Get up, Kasto! You still can't outwrestle me!"

Kasto was released and got to his feet. Gradually he started to make out the other boy's face.

"Limlan!" said Kasto. "What are you doing here?"

"I've been serving as a page here for most of a year," said Limlan. "I was excited to hear that you would be coming. I haven't seen you since the junior camp three years ago."

"I'm going back home to Druria in a few weeks," he continued. "But we'll have a great time together before I go."

He accompanied Kasto back to the stable yard to help carry the rest of his baggage. After they had brought it to the pages' room, Limlan showed Kasto where to put his clothes and weapons. When Kasto had finished unpacking, the boys sat down on their beds.

Kasto had never been on a bed before. At the farm and in the junior officers quarters, he had slept on straw mats on the ground. Here, the straw mat lay on a wood frame two feet above the ground. It was nice to be able to sit on the bed and not be on the ground, but Kasto secretly worried that he might fall off the bed at night when he was asleep.

"Pages' duties are easy," said Limlan. "We stay near Lord Damier at all times and perform whatever services he requires. Servants do most of the hard work, and we mainly just carry messages, find documents, and things like that. You'll catch on fast. The only hard part is dealing with Malvane, Lord Damier's son. He makes everyone call him 'Duke Malvane.' He thinks that being the king's nephew makes his blood more noble than ours. And he's only a year or so older than we are. I try to avoid his path as much as I can."

Chapter Three

Kasto did catch on fast. Lord Damier's palace and grounds were huge, almost as large as the royal palace back in Balarta. Hallways twisted past countless doorways, with side hallways leading to still other rooms. At times he could have used a cat like Amara's Shadenni to keep him from getting lost. Outdoors, passageways led from courtyard to courtyard, connecting stables to kitchens to barracks to the halls of the noble family. It would take time to learn all the mysteries of the palace, but after a couple of days he began to feel more comfortable in his surroundings. Limlan was always there to help him find his way to new places. For the first time, Kasto began to believe he could master living among the nobles.

It was in the late afternoon of his third day that he was walking through a dark corridor to deliver a message, trying to remember whether it was the second or third door on the right that he needed to find. An arm reached out of a doorway on the left and grabbed him by the tunic.

"Stop where you stand, common trash," said a nasty voice.

Kasto looked up to see a tall blond young man with hate written across his face.

"I know exactly what you are," the young man continued. "I overheard my father and the First Minister talking about you. I am disgusted at the sight of you wearing the colors of our distinguished family."

This must be Duke Malvane, thought Kasto.

"Imposters like you should go back to the gutters you came from," Malvane went on. "I would publicly reveal your deception, but it would be an embarrassment to my father and our king. Instead, I give you two days to resign your pageship and leave our household."

Kasto looked Malvane straight in the eyes. He was getting angry, but forced himself to remember his instructions to be polite and respectful in all situations. This was one of those situations.

"I regret that it will not be possible to obey your lordship's instructions," said Kasto. "It would bring dishonor on my king for me to leave my position here before the year is up."

Malvane tightened his grip on Kasto's tunic. "I promise you that every day you remain in this household will be the worst day of your pathetic little life," he said. "You'll wish you had never been born."

Kasto was on the verge of losing control of his temper.

"Thank you, your lordship," he was able to squeeze out. "I must continue on the errand that your father assigned to me."

He pushed past Malvane and went on down the corridor, shaking and turning white with rage. He swore to himself that no power on earth would keep him from finishing his year of pageship with success. *I must be strong,* he thought. *I must make Amara proud of me.* His back stiffened with determination.

*

Pages were allowed to participate in training sessions with the king's guards three times each week so that their skills in swordsmanship, archery, and other combat skills would not get rusty. Limlan took Kasto into the city streets and showed him the way to the quarters of the royal guard.

"I've been saving another surprise for you," said Limlan. "Wait till you meet the captain of the king's guards. You remember Namla from our training camp?"

"Of course," said Kasto. "He was the outstanding cadet at the camp."

"His ability has been recognized here in Holunland," said Limlan. "The captain of the guards was killed six months ago in a skirmish with the barbarians. Namla was chosen to be his replacement. I understand that he is the youngest man ever to serve as the captain."

"I am happy for Namla's success," said Kasto. "It will be good to see him."

They entered the gate of the royal guards barracks. Across the courtyard stood the squadron of junior officers, ready for the practice. At the right was Namla, wearing the uniform of a commander. He smiled at Kasto and held out his arms in greeting.

"Welcome, Kasto," he said. "It has been too long since we have been together."

Kasto greeted Namla in return, and prepared for the drill.

"Today you will be working with the wooden staffs," Namla instructed the men. "Each man get a staff, and ..."

He stopped suddenly, as two new arrivals entered the courtyard. Kasto turned to see Malvane and another man walking up to Namla, carrying staffs.

"We are indeed fortunate today," said Namla. "I see that Duke Malvane and his distinguished companion will be joining us." He turned back to the men. "After you have your staffs, form two lines facing each other and assume your positions of readiness."

He explained to Kasto, "Your first opponent will be the man facing you. When one man has scored three solid blows to his opponent's body, he has won, and combat will cease. The winner will move one place in my direction, the loser one place in the opposite direction. You then compete against the new man across from you. The one closest to me at the end will be the overall winner." He looked at Malvane's companion and smiled at the group. "Of course, today the winner will not be in question."

The men chuckled, and turned to choose partners and form the lines facing each other. They held their staffs upright with both hands in front of them. Kasto was facing one of the junior officers of the guards. It felt good to be in a familiar situation, one in which he excelled. He noticed that Malvane was next to him on his left side and Malvane's companion across from the man on his right, one place toward Namla..

"Begin combat!" ordered Namla.

The men moved forwards and back, feinting blows, parrying their opponents' blows, and launching blows of their own. Kasto was a swift and efficient fighter, quickly landing three solid hits on his opponent. When all the pairs had finished, he moved to his next position. Malvane and his friend both won easily also, so they moved along with him.

As the drill progressed, he moved farther and farther toward Namla. The older men progressed along with him, finding little difficulty with the younger officers. When he arrived at the end of the line, Kasto found himself standing next to Malvane and across from Malvane's companion.

Kasto heard a low whisper in his ear.

"Prepare to receive the beating of your life," hissed Malvane.

"Begin combat!" came the order.

Kasto's opponent was indeed much superior to the young men he had been facing. This man was a seasoned veteran of many bloody battles, as testified by the scars visible on his face and arms. They had scarcely started when Kasto was fooled by a feint, and his opponent landed a painful blow with the end of his staff into Kasto's ribs. Kasto gritted his teeth and came back to the ready position.

Combat began again. Not since his training sessions three years earlier with the traitor Simontor had Kasto met an opponent better with the staff than he was. Although he had no experience in actual battles, his strong, well-muscled body had been through years of training with the best instructors in the Eight Kingdoms. His swordsmanship battles with Amara had developed his quickness and reflexes, while his work with other officers had perfected his skills with other weapons. He had become the outstanding fighter in the Weltorian guards. Looking into his opponent's face with a smile, he settled himself for a long, difficult match. After much blocking and parrying, he was able to land a good blow to his opponent's torso with the side of his staff. His opponent smiled back at him. Each man now knew he was facing an opponent of the highest caliber.

It took several more minutes, but Kasto was able to penetrate his opponent's defense with another solid hit to the ribs. By now, all the other partnerships had finished and were watching, recognizing that they were seeing a battle between two experts.

Kasto felt himself beginning to tire, and he hoped his opponent was also getting weary. Trying to end the match quickly and take his opponent by surprise, he took a risk with a quick short poke directly to the midsection. Down came one end of the other man's staff, knocking Kasto's weapon toward the ground. The opposite end of the staff came quickly around, jarring into Kasto's ribs before he could recover.

The match was tied at two apiece. The other men had now formed a circle around the two combatants, cheering each good move made by either one of them. Kasto forced himself to be patient. He noticed that his opponent was also breathing heavily, showing signs of fatigue. They circled each other carefully, feinting again and again, but neither willing to attempt a true strike.

Kasto took a step to the side, and suddenly felt his feet go out from under him, as he stepped on something on the ground. As he stood helplessly flailing his arms, his opponent stepped forward and drew back his staff for the winning blow – but did not strike.

"I will not take advantage of an accident," he said, pointing to the ground under Kasto's feet. A staff had rolled out of the crowd and Kasto had stepped on it.

"He did it on purpose," shouted Limlan, pointing at Malvane, who stood empty-handed across the circle. "No one drops his staff by accident."

He ran toward Malvane, his staff at the ready. "I'll make you pay!"

Kasto grabbed Limlan halfway across the circle and held him tightly.

"I'm sure our lord duke would never intentionally interfere in another's combat," he said loudly. He whispered quietly into Limlan's ear, "Stop, as you're my friend. I'll explain later."

He turned to his opponent and held up his staff. "I'm ready now to resume our match."

The soldier stepped forward, holding out his empty hands. "I am willing to call our match even. It is not often that I come across my equal."

Kasto lowered his staff and shook the hands of his opponent. "Well fought," he said. "I do not think I would have gotten the third blow against you."

"Well spoken by both," said Namla. "I declare you to be equal winners of today's drill."

The crowd of young officers cheered the two winners and surrounded them with congratulations on their superb match. Out of the corner of his eye, Kasto saw Malvane going quietly out the courtyard gate, his face suffused with anger and hatred. If this was the beginning of his campaign against him, what could lie ahead? If only he could counsel with Amara. He felt far from home.

Later Limlan and Kasto walked through the streets on their way back to Lord Damier's palace.

"Do you know who that was that you were fighting against," asked Limlan.

Kasto shook his head. "I know only that he is the equal of any of the instructors at the academy."

"He is the champion staffsman of the entire Holunland army," said Limlan. "Malvane must brought him today for the sole purpose of humiliating you, injuring you if possible. When the battle was even, he rolled his staff under your feet to make sure you would lose. I saw his face fill with hatred whenever he looked at you. What has made him such an enemy of yours?"

"Tonight, when we go to bed in our quarters, I will explain," answered Kasto.

*

After darkness came, Kasto and Limlan undressed and wrapped their blankets around themselves on their beds. Kasto knew he could no longer put off giving Limlan his explanation.

"It has been important to me to have your friendship," he began. "What I must now tell you will put an end to that friendship."

"I do not think so," said Limlan. "My bond of friendship is not so easily broken."

Kasto started again. "I must tell you that my father is a great man in my country. He has been chosen to be our king's Royal Minister of Farming. Our family owns one of the largest farms in Weltoria."

"Many people own farms," said Limlan. "Why should that cause Malvane to hate you so much?"

"Although my father is a Royal Minister, he is not of the nobility. He is a commoner, and so am I. I am pretending to be something that I am not." Kasto's voice choked. "That is why Malvane hates me, and now you will hate me also."

Silence fell on their chamber. Kasto curled around himself in his bed, trying to keep himself from sobbing in front of Limlan. He was all alone, far from the love and support of Amara. He was now losing his only true friend in all of Holunland. Then he was surprised to hear Limlan laughing.

"What a little thing for you to worry about," said Limlan. "Noble blood is much more important to commoners than it is to most nobles. What you should understand is that all noble families were once commoners themselves. Some time in the past, one of their ancestors performed a service to the king, and was raised to the nobility in gratitude.

"My great-great grandfather showed great bravery in battle, and saved his king's life. That is how I come to have noble blood."

Kasto thought about this. "So you don't despise me?" he asked.

"Of course not. You're the same Kasto and I'm the same Limlan that we were an hour ago. We're still friends."

Kasto rubbed the tears from his eyes and cleared his throat. "Your friendship is important," he said. "The next weeks will be difficult for me."

*

The next two weeks, however, went easily for Kasto. He was now comfortable in his position, and he managed to keep out of Malvane's path as much as possible. In public, especially in front of his father, Malvane showed nothing but extreme courtesy toward Kasto. Kasto was fully on his guard at all times, but Malvane seemed to be ignoring him.

At the end of the second week, a special treat was in store for the pages. Bardloro knocked at the door of their chamber as they were preparing for sleep.

"His Lordship has sent a message for you," he announced. "You are to attend tomorrow night's banquet and ball as invited guests."

The boys were excited. Kasto spent the whole next day remembering his instruction in dining and dancing at formal occasions. This would be his first test. When evening came, he hoped he was ready.

The lowest-ranking guests were supposed to be the first to arrive at Lord Damier's banquets. Kasto and Limlan made sure that they were the earliest. Kasto had never attended banquets in Balarta. He found the luxury of the setting almost impossible to believe.

The banquet hall was hung with bright tapestries, and the air shimmered with the light from dozens of candelabra. The U-shaped banquet table was covered with lush cloths, on which were gold and silver goblets and eating implements. Kasto hoped he would remember which implements should be used for which courses. Seats for Lord and Lady Damier were at the head of the table, with the highest-ranking guests seated near them on both sides. The lowest ranking guests were at the two ends of the table and were the first to stand behind their places.

Kasto and Limlan were placed together at the very end of the table. They stood as they watched the other guests enter, taking their places in turn. When there were only two places remaining, Lord and Lady Damier entered, greeted by applause from their guests. When the hosts had seated themselves, the guests were then free to take their own chairs.

Course after course appeared, carried on platters by brightly dressed servants. Pitchers of wine flowed freely into goblets, and before long the company had become quite merry. Kasto was tempted to sample the wine, but his experience at the tavern was too recent for him to yield to this temptation. He had prepared for his thirst by drinking great quantities of spring water before coming to the hall.

Next to him, Limlan sipped his wine, but did not drain his goblet over and over again as most of the guests were doing. Both of the pages were careful to restrain themselves while eating the rich food. Every dish provided a new taste to Kasto, and he wanted to sample them all without becoming sick. He saw some of the guests leaving the room every now and then, coming back with pasty faces.

"They're going out to empty their stomachs," explained Limlan. "It's disgusting."

The banquet finally came to an end. Lord Damier rose in his place.

"Let us dance," he said. He and Lady Damier led the guests into the next hall, where an orchestra was waiting.

Many of the guests seemed barely able to stagger into the dancing room after their drinking and eating at the banquet. But Kasto was surprised to see them take to the dance floor with ease and flow gracefully across the room in perfect time with the music. He and Limlan stayed near the wall for the first three dances. Kasto dreaded the moment when he would have to expose his lack of dancing ability to all. Limlan nudged him.

"See the two young ladies over there?" he said. "Let us ask them for the next dance."

Kasto summoned up courage and nodded his head, and they offered their hands to the girls. As the orchestra began playing the next dance, Kasto found himself whirling around the hall with a beautiful partner. *This is certainly different from dancing with my teacher back in Weltoria,* he thought.

The dance steps were familiar to him, but performing them and keeping off his partner's toes in a room full of other couples all moving at full speed was tricky. He remembered to give his partner his nicest smiles whenever they faced each other. He was just beginning to feel confident with his dancing when another dancer's body slammed into him from behind. Kasto was knocked into his partner, and the two of them went down in a heap on the floor. The couples around them halted in their places, and the orchestra stopped playing.

Kasto looked up at the circle of faces around him. He started to rise and apologize to his partner when an insolent voice cut through the silence.

"Those who cannot control their use of the wine goblet should know better than to try to dance with young ladies," said Malvane, stepping forward from the circle. He held out his hand to the girl on the floor. "Please allow me to apologize for the disgusting drunkenness of my father's page."

Limlan jumped into the circle.

"That's a lie," he shouted. "I sat with Kasto at the banquet table, and no wine at all touched his lips. You must have pushed him down yourself."

Malvane smiled at the circle of guests. "Whatever reason could I have for doing such an unlikely thing?" he said. "It is loyal of you to stand behind your fellow page, but the evidence of his drunken behavior speaks for itself."

Limlan stepped toward Malvane in anger, but by now Kasto was on his feet and stepped between them.

"I must apologize for my clumsiness," he said to his partner, then turned to Malvane. "I do not, in fact, take liquor," he said. "But I can understand how my ineptness at dancing would lead your lordship to believe that I had taken too much."

He bowed to Malvane, took Limlan by the arm, and left the hall.

Chapter Four

The next morning, Kasto had reported for duty and was standing in his usual position two paces behind Lord Damier's right shoulder when the lord turned to face him.

"I must apologize for my son's actions toward you last evening," he said. "As our page, you are a guest in our household. Although Duke Malvane was extremely concerned over possible injury to the young lady, he should not have accused you of drunkenness. Sometimes he carries the virtues of chivalry to excess."

Damier paused, then continued. "I had hoped that you and Malvane would grow to be friends. In many ways, he represents the finest qualities of our Holunland nobility, qualities that a young man in your position would do well to emulate."

Kasto bowed. "Yes, your lordship," he said.

"I have an assignment that will allow the two of you to become better acquainted," said Damier, holding up a letter in his hand. "I have received reports of a panther that has been terrorizing villages on my estates in the eastern part of our country. Both you and Malvane are extremely capable at arms, and I have decided to send you to dispose of the rogue beast. You may now pack your needs for the journey, you shall depart this afternoon."

He dismissed Kasto, who returned to his quarters to begin packing. Fate was not on his side, he thought. Spending several days alone with his enemy was the worst prospect he could imagine. Limlan was not sympathetic.

"You should have let me go at Malvane when I had the chance. Now you must make sure your back is never turned on him. He's capable of any sort of treachery you could imagine."

"I'll be careful," said Kasto. "I don't think he'll do anything openly. He'll try to make me lose my temper with his constant abuse, to put me in the wrong for whatever he has planned."

*

The abuse started as soon as the two men had left the city gate and crossed the moat.

"I want you always two horse-lengths behind me," ordered Malvane. "It's bad enough having to endure your stench for several days. I don't want your filth dirtying my horse or my packs."

"Yes, whatever your lordship wishes, your lordship," said Kasto. He could play the game as easily as Malvane could.

After two days on the road, they arrived at a tiny village in the hills not far from the eastern border. It consisted of no more than a dozen huts surrounded by tiny fields in the midst of a forest.

"Wait here," ordered Malvane. "I don't want to insult my father's villagers with your revolting presence."

He dismounted and entered the village. Kasto heard the village chief telling Malvane about the panther.

"It has been carrying off our animals," he said. "We tried to dispose of it ourselves, but it killed two of our men. Now that it has tasted human flesh, we are afraid to let our children play outdoors."

He gave Malvane directions to the area where the panther had its den, and thanked him for coming to protect them. Malvane came back to Kasto.

"It is too late in the day for panther-hunting," he said. "I shall go after the beast in the morning. I shall expect you to stay well out of my way. This will be a difficult hunt and I cannot allow you to make mistakes that would make things harder for me."

"As your lordship wishes, your lordship," said Kasto. He had the satisfaction of seeing Malvane grit his teeth in frustration.

*

They began their hunt early the next morning on horseback.

"The only reason I am allowing you to accompany me is to help in carrying back the dead animal," said Malvane. "It will make an excellent trophy for my father's hunting lodge."

They followed the directions the village chief had given them. The landscape was gently rolling hills, some with patches of forest, but mostly low bushes for land cover. As they neared the crest of a hill, Malvane held up his hand. He dismounted and signaled for Kasto to do likewise.

"According to the chief, we should be able to see the beast's den from the top of this hill," he said in a low voice.

They crept carefully to the crest and peered over the top. By straining his eyes, Kasto could, in the distance, just make out the panther lying in front of a cave next to a dry streambed. What appeared to be the remains of a partly eaten antelope lay next to the big cat. Malvane pulled Kasto back from the hilltop.

"I will now go to kill the panther," he said. He took off his sword and dagger and hung them on his saddle. "These might make noise and alert my prey. Hold the horses here for me and be sure not to make any noise."

He moved quietly over the hilltop, carrying only his bow and arrows. *If Amara were here, she would be able to hit the animal from this distance*, thought Kasto. He peered over the hill, watching Malvane move carefully through the rocks and bushes, always keeping out of the cat's vision. Patiently, Malvane moved ever closer to his target without making the slightest sound. Kasto had to respect Malvane's stalking ability. His enemy was clearly an expert hunter.

Finally Malvane was close enough to the panther to get a good shot. He stood up from behind the boulder that concealed him, drew his bow, and made a perfect shot. The panther roared, jumped up straight in the air, and landed in a heap. It tried to drag itself to cover, but could manage only a short distance before it collapsed and lay still.

Malvane notched another arrow in his bow and approached the animal carefully. Hunters had been maimed by animals they thought were dead, but Malvane was obviously too experienced to take a chance. When he was near enough to the panther, he shot the second arrow into its neck at pointblank range. He then waved his hands over his head, signaling Kasto to bring the horses.

Before Kasto could mount, his eyes widened in horror. Three horsemen dressed in animal skins were riding sturdy ponies at full speed up the creek bed from the opposite direction. He saw Malvane lift his head and see them, but before he could notch an arrow and shoot, they were upon him. One of them, without stopping his horse, jumped onto Malvane, knocking him to the ground. The other two pulled up, and the three of them were quickly able to subdue his struggles and bind his arms and legs.

The three of them talked for a moment, then scanned the horizon in all directions. Kasto felt their eyes pass over his hiding place on the hilltop, but they moved on without showing any sign of having seen him.

The three barbarians tied the panther over the rear of one of their ponies and Malvane over the rear of another one. They remounted and headed back in the direction they had come from.

In a short few minutes, all Kasto's problems had been solved. Not only would his enemy be gone forever, but the thought of the haughty Malvane spending the rest of his life as a slave in a barbarian village would keep him warm for many a cold night. He needed only to ride back to the village and report the sad event. Kasto stood up, mounted his horse and began to ride—in pursuit of the barbarians.

From his studies of the geography of Holunland, he knew that they must be very close to the border. He would not have much time to catch up to the savages before they entered their own country. This must have been a scouting party preparing for a raid. The main barbarian force would not be far away.

He took his horse down the hilltop and reached the dry streambed. Riding as fast as he could, he soon passed the panther's den. The small barbarian ponies were sturdy, but they were now carrying heavy burdens and would have to travel slowly. Kasto planned his attack. There were three of them to his one, but the only weapons they carried were large, clumsy sabers. He felt confident that he could take on all three at once.

He rounded a turn in the streambed, and between the trees on both sides of it he could see the three riders in front of him. He spurred on his horse. As he drew closer, the barbarians stopped and looked behind them. Seeing only one rider, they didn't seem worried. The three of them dismounted and stood side-by-side, blocking Kasto's path.

Kasto pulled up his horse and also dismounted. The barbarians had their swords out, high and ready to swing. Kasto drew his sword with his right hand and his dagger with his left. As he stepped forward, the barbarians laughed and started to encircle him. When they had formed a triangle with him at the center, the one facing him took a huge swing with his saber. Kasto easily dodged it and struck straight with his sword, right through the barbarian's ribs and out the back of his torso. The man collapsed and Kasto immediately tried to whirl to face his other two opponents.

His sword was stuck in the dead man's body, and before Kasto could pull it back out, he felt a shock to his right shoulder, and his sword arm no longer worked. He turned to see the third attacker beginning his swing and was able to duck under it. Dropping the dagger to the ground, he jerked his sword from the dead man's body with his left hand and backed off to face the two attackers.

Even with his right arm now hanging uselessly at his side, Kasto was too well trained in combat to have difficulty matching the two barbarians clumsily swinging their sabers. He let another swing go by him, then stepped close to the attacker's body and plunged his sword into the man's heart. He instantly turned to face the third man, who had had enough combat and was running for the unladen pony. Kasto heard him ride into the distance as he cut Malvane's ropes.

Malvane slid off the pony's back and looked at Kasto. For once, he seemed to be without words. Then he pulled himself to his full height.

"I can hardly go back to my family and friends with the humiliation of having been saved by a deceitful peasant. It would be better to have died."

Kasto looked Malvane in the eyes. "There are only two witnesses to today's events," he said. "I promise you that I would never contradict your lordship's report of them."

Malvane sniffed haughtily. "I suppose I must dirty my hands in binding that wound," he said. "Try to keep from getting any more of your low blood on me than is necessary."

Kasto looked down at his right shoulder and was sickened. The fire of battle was wearing off, and he could see the meat of his arm hanging open when the saber had sliced into it. Pain began to seep into his consciousness. Malvane tore a strip of cloth from his own jacket and bound Kasto's arm back together as tightly as possible. He helped Kasto back onto his horse and led it to the hilltop where his own horse was tethered. They rode back to the village side by side, Malvane making sure Kasto did not fall from his horse.

By the time they arrived at the village, Kasto was barely conscious due to pain and loss of blood. He later vaguely remembered his wound being unbound, reopened, and having water poured over it. Then all went black.

When he woke up, he was lying on a bed in a stone room. His shoulder was tied to a wooden brace so that he couldn't move it at all. A dull ache had replaced the intense pain. No one seemed to be nearby.

"Where am I?" he croaked, as loudly as he could. In a few minutes, a head appeared in the doorway.

"Well, our young barbarian-fighter has come back to the world."

A man entered the room, wearing the uniform of the Holunian army.

"Where am I?" Kasto tried again.

"This is a fortified border post," said the man. "A base that our army uses for its patrols against the barbarians."

"Did Duke Malvane bring me?" Kasto asked.

"He brought you into the post yesterday, tied to the back of your horse. You looked more dead than alive, but we have much experience here of wounds from barbarian sabers. They are clumsy weapons, but they are sharp and leave clean wounds. I have put men back together who were cut apart much worse than you are."

"My arm," said Kasto. "Will I... " His voice dropped off. *Never to be able to use a sword again? How could he serve and protect Amara?* Her face appeared in his mind, but he was afraid to think about her. He looked up at the healer.

"Your arm will heal nicely. In my experience, which is considerable, limbs frequently are even stronger after healing than they were before the wound. In six months time you will be a better swordsman than ever."

Chapter Five

Kasto spent three weeks in the post infirmary, his arm in the brace. His bandages were changed every day, his wound was covered with healing medicines, and he was fed a diet loaded with meat to help his muscles knit strongly. At the end of the three weeks, he was declared ready to return to the capital, his arm in a sling.

"You must keep your arm in the sling for another three weeks. You will be tempted to test it before that time, but you must resist. Remember, if you can be patient, it will be stronger than ever."

It was late afternoon when Kasto rode back into Lord Damier's palace grounds. Bardloro helped him stable his horse and carry his pack to the pages' quarters.

"Lord Damier wishes to see you early in the morning," Bardloro told him. "It would be unwise to be late."

Kasto entered the pages' quarters and looked around for Limlan. The room was dark, but Kasto could see that all of Limlan's belongings were gone. On his bed was a piece of paper. Kasto took it to the window. It was a farewell note. Limlan's term as page had ended and he had returned to his country. Kasto sank onto his own bed. His best friend in Holunland was gone, he had a useless arm, and he had still ten months to endure Malvane's torments.

I can't feel sorry for myself, he told himself, and fell asleep trying to believe it.

*

Morning came soon. He jumped out of bed and dressed himself in his page's uniform. He would feel conspicuous wearing his sling, and for a moment considered not wearing it. Then he remembered the healer's words and put it on.

He entered Lord Damier's chamber, bowed and looked up in surprise. Sitting in council with Lord Damier were the king, the First Minister, and Duke Malvane. Kasto bowed again, hastily, to the king.

"Arise," said the king. "We are pleased to welcome you back to our capital city. We are anxious to hear the story of your wound."

The First Minister spoke next. "We understand that you were set upon and wounded by three barbarians. Duke Malvane then came to your rescue and routed them. Is this correct?"

Kasto looked at Malvane, whose face was expressionless. He turned back to the king and First Minister. He had prepared himself for this moment the entire time he had been healing.

"That is correct, sir," he said, speaking with military precision.

The king, First Minister, and Lord Damier all looked at each other. Lord Damier was the first to speak.

"You should be aware, young man," he said, "that honesty is a quality highly prized in our country. I feel that you demonstrate yourself to be somewhat lacking in that regard."

"However," said the king, "honor is even more highly prized, and you do demonstrate yourself to be well endowed with that quality."

By now, Kasto was totally confused. He had given the right answer, what was happening? The king continued. "My nephew, Duke Malvane, has told a somewhat different version of the events in question. According to him, he had been captured by the three barbarians and was being carried off into slavery. You gave pursuit, and without regard for your own safety, you attacked, killing two of them and routing the third. You did this even after receiving your bitter wound. What say you to this account?"

Kasto was speechless. Malvane came to his rescue.

"I have given this matter much thought. I cannot approve of your deceit in pretending to have noble blood. But my own honor requires nothing less than a completely true account of my rescue." He looked intensely at Kasto. "I owe you my life in freedom," he said stiffly. "For that I must give you my thanks."

He rose and left the chamber.

"I echo his thanks," said Lord Damier. "It appears that our decision to allow you to serve as our page was a wise one. You may return to your duties."

Kasto's head was whirling for the rest of the day. He didn't notice the way he was looked at by everyone he passed in the course of his duties, nor that there were preparations in the air for a special occasion. This first day back was exhausting, and he fell into a deep and refreshing sleep as soon as he lay down in his bed.

*

In the morning, he was awakened by Bardloro shaking him roughly.

"Put on your finest dress uniform immediately," said Bardloro. "I will await you in the courtyard.

Kasto hurried did as he had been told and joined Bardloro, who led him into the streets outside the lord's palace. They walked toward the royal palace, entered its grounds, and went to the royal temple. Bardloro took him to a side entrance and told him to wait for instructions. After a short wait, two senior officers in full dress uniform opened the entrance and led him into the temple.

They crossed the temple's main hall and entered a small chapel at the side. Candlelight filled the chapel. Kasto looked around and saw the king seated in front of the altar, with three priests, the First Minister, and Lord Damier standing at his sides. Malvane, Namla, and other young officers stood at the side of the chapel. The king beckoned Kasto to come forward. He stood before the king and bowed deeply.

"In recognition of your bravery in saving the life of my royal nephew," said the king, "we wish to provide you with an appropriate reward. Bravery itself, however, is not a sufficient quality for the award you are to receive. The purpose of our meeting with you yesterday was to assure us that you also embody the highest ideal of a gentleman, that of honor. It is my pleasure to recognize officially the noble qualities you have demonstrated."

He stood up. "I command you, Count Kasto of Vernoria, to rise and accept this ennoblement."

Kasto stood up. He had no idea what to say, but as he started to mumble his gratitude the First Minister began to speak.

"Your estate in our province Vernoria will consist of two villages and their surrounding farms, of which Lord Damier has assigned you the titles. Lord Damier's overseers will manage the property on your behalf, and you will receive the profits from the lands." He cleared his throat. "After, of course, the taxes due to His Majesty the King have been deducted."

The nobles chuckled. Now it was Kasto's turn to speak. His mind had been racing throughout the ceremony. He squared his shoulders.

"I regret, Your Majesty, that I have not the appropriate words to thank you for these honors," he said. "I can only promise you that I will try my best to prove myself worthy of them."

"I am certain that you shall be," said the king. He stepped forward, followed by the nobles and the young officers with their hands extended in congratulations.

*

Kasto was in a daze for the rest of the day, and for most of the following week. He was still a page, and all of the important dignitaries visiting Lord Damier had far higher rank in the nobility than he did. But he no longer felt an outsider hiding a secret from the world. Even Malvane, while still reserved, no longer treated him with open disdain.

Before long, messages of congratulations began arriving. King Taran and Queen Asuma wrote to express their delight at the heroism of their subject. First Minister Rabak was pleased with his good judgment in sending Kasto to Holunland. Limlan wrote from Druria to complain that he had missed all the excitement. Kasto's parents were happy that their son's noble character had finally been recognized. Finally, the letter arrived that Kasto most been hoping for.

My dear Count Kasto, it began. How nice that sounds! I think however, that I shall continue to call you simply Kasto. You have never called me anything other than Amara. We haven't changed since we were two little children playing in the mud and dust of your father's fields. I hope we never lose that feeling for as long as we live. I look forward to spending the rest of my life with you.

Your best friend, Amara.

Chronicle the Fifth
Royal Wedding

Chapter One

"You never let me have a fair chance at Kasto," teased Zismelda. "You kept him all to yourself."

She was sitting in Amara's bedchamber, brushing Amara's long, light-brown locks. Hundreds of strokes with the silver-and-bone brush were bringing an iridescent sheen to the bride-to-be's hair. Amara sat impatiently, her cat Shadenni on her lap, waiting for the torture to end.

The royal wedding of Princess Amara of Weltoria to Count Kasto of Vernoria was only four weeks away. Her parents, King Taran and Queen Asuma, were delighted that circumstances had transpired three years earlier to ennoble Kasto and thus make him an eligible candidate for marriage to a princess. Count Kasto had dedicated his life to serving Amara and her parents and was the ideal man for his future role as Prince Consort when Amara would someday become Queen.

Zismelda continued, "He's the best-looking man in both the twin kingdoms, maybe in all the Eight Kingdoms. I think you should have at least let me spend some time at court with him." Without changing a beat in her brushstrokes, she went on, "Your hair is gorgeous. You'll be the most beautiful bride in history. I love the colors of the gowns you've chosen for your attendants. The pink will show off my dark hair to good effect, don't you think?"

A smile covered Amara's face. An outsider listening to Zismelda's chatter would be certain that she was nothing more than she seemed, a silly young noblewoman with nothing more in her head than handsome young men, fashionable clothing, parties and balls. But that outsider would be very mistaken. Although Zismelda did, in fact, enjoy parties and handsome young men, under her surface veneer was hidden a trained warrior, deadly in armed combat.

"You'll be the most beautiful matron-of-honor in history, no matter what color you wear," said Amara, grimacing as Zismelda gave her a particularly painful brushstroke.

Amara had visited her cousin in Laritia for two months each autumn since their time together five years earlier at the elite training academy. The two young women had trained together in fighting skills on those visits. Zismelda had been nearly her equal in archery at the camp and had now built herself into the best archer in the Twin Kingdoms. Amara had to admit that as they had grown older, Zismelda had surpassed her in all aspects of combat.

Officially, Zismelda would be her matron of honor at the royal wedding, but with less than a month to go before the big event, her principal role was now to serve secretly as Amara's bodyguard.

As Zismelda finished the last strokes, Amara tossed her hair and turned.

"You've a very handsome husband, yourself," she said. "When you married Rangoto you broke the heart of half the maidens in the Eight Kingdoms."

Zismelda's husband, a wealthy nobleman in his late twenties, was indeed handsome, and Zismelda was deeply in love with him.

"Since your parents announced your engagement to Kasto last year, there was nothing left for me than to settle for Rangoto," she said. "I must admit that he does an excellent job of helping me forget my crush on your intended."

"I find that since our wedding announcement was made, I have difficulty keeping up my own crush on my intended," said Amara. "For the sake of preventing rumors about our relationship, we must no longer meet in person. The only times I get to see him are across the room at official occasions."

Zismelda laughed, and Amara joined her. It was important to keep their spirits high with all the tensions that the next month would bring. Security precautions were at their maximum level. Enemies of Amara's father would need to act quickly if they were to prevent Amara's marriage and the children it would bring. With three generations of Taran's line all living, it would be almost impossible for usurpers to depose him and claim the throne. But if Amara could somehow be eliminated before producing heirs, her father's reign would be in extreme jeopardy.

The two young women checked their appearance. Their flowing robes obscured the outline of the daggers they each wore at their waists. Finding themselves suitable for public view, they left the chamber for the public rooms of the royal palace.

*

Late that evening, darkness shrouded the palace as Amara slid from under her sheets. She tiptoed across her chamber and peeked into the antechamber, where Zismelda had her bed. After making sure that Zismelda was asleep, Amara slipped quietly across the antechamber, pulled back the bolt on the door, and stepped out into a corridor. Amara knew the palace by heart, and in the total blackness of night she found her way to a little-used storeroom. She entered the room and felt her way across it to a stack of boxes. Behind the stack she found what she was searching for.

Moments later, if there had been light in the corridor, a watcher would have seen a peasant girl dressed in drab brown clothing leave the storeroom that a princess had entered shortly before. The peasant girl walked through the dark hallways to a small side door to the palace. This door was used by palace servants and other employees to come and go without having to appear at the main palace gates. The doorway was small enough to be easily defended by a few members of the palace guard.

The guards on night duty had been instructed by Princess Amara that they were to allow free passage to this particular peasant girl, at all hours of day or night, and further ordered to keep these instructions secret, even from other members of the guard. It was not for humble soldiers to question commands from a royal princess, so they allowed the peasant girl to leave the palace and locked the door firmly behind her.

Amara would frequently use this route to take temporary leave from her role as a princess and visit her friends among the common people. On this particular night, however, she had another purpose. Since her childhood, she had always listened to the watervoices in the river when she needed information about the future. Although the events prophesied by the watervoices always came to pass, unfortunately it was usually difficult for Amara to decipher the meaning of their song. Tonight she was so concerned about what dangers the next month might bring that she was willing to risk a visit to the river.

She was so concerned, in fact, that she did not notice a small group of men watching the palace, men who saw the peasant girl leave the side exit, men whose patience had been rewarded. As one man hurried to report their observation to their superiors, the rest of the band followed Amara silently through the city.

Winds blustered between the buildings, and Amara wrapped her cloak more tightly around her to protect herself from the cold. There was barely enough light coming from the night sky for her to find her way through the dark streets to the edge of the city and to the river beyond. As she entered the tall grass at the river's edge, she saw a shimmering glow from beneath the surface of the water.

She seated herself on the grass and listened carefully. The wind blew even stronger along the river, and the rustling of reeds made it hard to hear anything. Softly, very softly, the piping of watervoices came from the depths, muffled by the wind.

> *Wedding to come, danger ---------,*
> *Too late to -------------.*
> *Talking will fail, brave men will quail*
> *----------------- evil's force.*

Danger? Evil? She strained her ears, almost afraid to listen to what she might hear. The winds abated briefly and she could hear clearly.

> *Wedding to come, danger for one,*
> *Too late to alter its course.*
> *Talking will fail, brave men will quail*
> *Nothing can stop evil's force.*

Amara was worried. This was the prophecy she had hoped not to hear. The voices continued.

In a dungeon's dark hole, a princess ----
Is to strive -------------

She didn't want to believe what she was hearing. The rustling of reeds and bushes was louder now, and she could barely hear the watervoices.

The bride will not be --------

What were they trying to tell her? What would she not be? Then a lull came in the wind, and she could hear again.

In a dungeon's dark hole, a princess's role
Is to strive to regain freedom's flame.
Though sword strokes be made, and magic may aid,
The bride will not be the same.

She was not to be the bride? Amara refused to let herself believe the prophecy. She shook her head and puzzled over the meaning of the watervoices. The howling of the wind returned, muffling rough footsteps that came toward her.

She felt herself seized by strong hands. Her sword arm reached for her dagger, but her adversaries held it firmly. She jerked it loose, drew the dagger, and stabbed blindly into the dark. A cry of pain, followed by curses, rewarded her effort.

Her attackers redoubled their efforts and their strength of numbers overpowered her. She was crushed face down on the ground, a heavy boot on her sword arm. A cloth was tied around her face to prevent her from calling for help. She felt the sleeve being pushed up her left arm.

"The scar is here," a rough voice said. "This is the one we seek."

Amara felt a sack being placed over her head. Sickly-sweet fumes filled her nose and throat, and total darkness descended on her.

*

The next morning, Zismelda yawned and stretched in bed. Light poured from the chamber windows. Strange. Amara usually would have been pestering her by this time, waking her from her beauty sleep to get ready for breakfast and the coming day. Zismelda jumped from bed and hurried to Amara's chamber. Looking inside, she saw an empty bed and no one in the room. Shadenni was missing as well. Zismelda looked back into her own chamber and saw that the door to the corridor was unbolted.

This is not good, she thought. Amara should not have left the chamber without Zismelda to accompany her. She rang for the maid.

"Princess Amara is sleeping late this morning," she told her. "Make sure that she is not disturbed until I return."

She talked yesterday about not being able to meet with Kasto, she thought. *Maybe they have a secret rendezvous.*

She walked briskly to the officers' quarters, hoping to find that Kasto was missing.

"Is Count Kasto here?" she asked soldier at the gate to the compound.

"Yes, your ladyship," he replied. "I believe he is training with Lord Limlan. I will summon him immediately."

Limlan, Kasto's friend since the days of the youth training camps, had fought side-by-side with Kasto in the past three years. He had traveled from his homeland of Druria to stand by Kasto in the days before the wedding.

He and Kasto ran to the gate. "How is my lady Zismelda?" he began, but broke off when he saw the expression on her face.

Kasto immediately grew worried. "What brings you?" he asked.

"Come with me," she answered. "We need to meet with the king and queen."

"I must leave you here," said Kasto to Limlan. He turned and crossed the courtyard with Zismelda.

As they hurried to the royal chambers, Zismelda explained her worries to Kasto. Kasto grew even more solemn.

King Taran and Queen Asuma were in their antechamber finishing their breakfast. Taran looked up in surprise when the two young people burst into the room. He dismissed the servants from the chamber and sent for Asuma's brother, the First Minister Rabak. After hearing Zismelda's report, he thought for a while before speaking.

"Our first job will be to make sure that she is actually missing, not simply occupied with wedding preparations or other duties somewhere in the palace. I don't think she will be found here, but we must eliminate that possibility before we go on.

You did right in coming directly to us without raising an alarm. If our daughter is missing, we must keep this secret for the present time."

Taran continued, "Kasto, you and Zismelda go separately and look through the palace in all the places she might possibly be found. Report back here as soon as you finish. The queen, the First Minister, and I will be making plans for the next steps while you are gone."

Kasto and Zismelda bowed and began their search of the palace. Kasto covered the stables, kitchens, and all the outbuildings. Zismelda searched the public rooms and the private royal suites. Within half an hour, both had returned to the royal chamber, unsuccessful in their missions. After they had reported, Rabak stood up and faced them.

"It is crucial that this news remain secret for now," he said. "Amara is so popular with the people of our country that extreme unrest could arise if any suspicion that evil has befallen her becomes public."

He continued, "We will have a closed coach, accompanied by her personal maids and servants, leave later this morning for our palace in the country. You, Zismelda, will lead a squadron of troops to accompany it. We shall let it be known that Amara will be spending the next two weeks there, resting for the busy days before the wedding. I want you to return here at nightfall, under the strictest cloak of secrecy."

He turned to Kasto. "You will remain here for the present. I have activated my network of observers throughout the kingdom, and if we receive any report of her, you will lead the palace guards to the rescue. For the time being, we must all wait."

Kasto's fists were clenched tightly in frustration and his face was flushed with anger, but he bowed his head to King Taran and remained silent.

Chapter Two

By midmorning of the following day, no reports had yet been received. Kasto paced impatiently back and forth in the royal chambers. Zismelda sat near the king and queen and watched Kasto's brooding face, the redness of his tell-tale scars revealing his feelings. In the past three years, all traces of boyhood had vanished from his appearance. Hordes of barbarians had mounted a major invasion of eastern Holunland, and forces from all of the Eight Kingdoms had gathered to resist their advance. Kasto, with a debt to settle against the barbarians, had led the armies of Weltoria and Laritia into battle. He had seen comrades fall in combat – his close friend Rontes had died in his arms – and his own face and body were covered with scars. It had taken over two years of steady fighting to destroy the invading forces, and Kasto had been home for only two months.

The tension was broken by a knock at the door, followed by the entry of Rabak, accompanied by a messenger. The messenger bowed to the king.

"Your Majesty, our observers have seen a large group of armed men riding hard along the northern road. They were guarding a black carriage with closed window curtains."

Taran looked questioningly at Rabak. Rabak nodded.

"Their destination appears to be Intor Castle," he said.

Intor Castle was a powerful fortress located in the mountainous lands at the far northern part of Weltoria. The Duke of Intor was one of the most influential men in the kingdom, and his influence seemed always to be directed against King Taran and his family. The duke's cousins Maleviol and Namintor had led a coup that had murdered Taran's predecessor, and they had been executed by Taran as soon as he was crowned king.

The duke had sworn loyalty to Taran, and Taran had trusted him until his nephew Simontor had almost succeeded in assassinating Amara. After she had killed him in self-defense the hatred of the House of Intor was directed toward her as well as her father.

"We must act swiftly, but silently," said Taran. "If our daughter is still alive, they may kill her if they find themselves threatened. Kasto, take command of the entire force of Watchful Ones and Palace Guards. At nightfall, lead them north, but not in a direct route to Intor. Position yourselves within striking distance of Intor Castle, but out of sight in the forest. I will join you as soon as we obtain more definite information."

Zismelda stood up before the king. "I beg permission to accompany the forces," she said. "I must make amends for my failure to protect my princess."

"You have no blame for our daughter's disappearance," said Asuma. "We are certain that she, herself, eluded your protection for reasons of her own. Do not assume guilt for what is not your responsibility."

"I think I understand our niece's feelings," added Taran. "You may join the contingent led by Kasto."

"Thank you, Your Majesty," said Zismelda. She and Kasto bowed to the king and queen, and left the chamber.

*

Far to the north, consciousness slowly returned to Amara, lying in a dungeon cell in the depths of Intor Castle. She stayed motionless and opened her eyes a crack, to see where she was. Bars covered the cell's door to a corridor. A guard was sitting outside.

A surge of guilt swept over her. Why had she let her curiosity overcome her? Now she was a prisoner of her family's enemies, a pawn to be used as a hostage against her father. The watervoices' prophecy echoed bitterly in her head:

> *Talking will fail, brave men will quail*
> *Nothing can stop evil's force.*

There was to be no way to spare her life, neither negotiations nor fighting. She kept herself from sobbing, but she felt all alone and helpless. What else had they said?

> *Though sword strokes be made, and magic may aid,*
> *The bride will not be the same.*

No matter what could be done to help her, nothing could stop the forces against her. Someday Kasto would be married to another girl. Even the magical cat Shadenni, who had saved her life many times, seemed to have deserted her.

As dark waves of gloom seemed about to drown her, she remembered who she was. Royal Princess Amara, daughter of King Taran, heir to the throne of the Twin Kingdoms of Weltoria and Laritia, and fiancée of Count Kasto of Vernoria. Defeat was not a possibility she could accept. As she lay quietly, pretending still to be unconscious, a plan began to form in her head.

Outside her cell, a young soldier sat in the corridor. He wondered why so much importance had been placed on his guarding the peasant girl who lay sleeping in the cell. He had been warned that she was a powerful witch. The key to her cell door was tied to his belt, and he had been ordered to guard her carefully, and to keep his hand tight on his sword at all times.

He watched her through the bars of the cell. The girl didn't look like a witch to him. Her face was young and innocent as she slept peacefully. Surely some kind of mistake had been made. He leaned back in his seat and occupied himself by counting the cracks in the ceiling.

Had he been more watchful, he would have seen the girl's eyelids open cautiously. He would have seen her lying motionless, only her eyes darting around the dungeon, noting the location of the door and of his seat. Had he listened more carefully, he would have heard her whispering words under her breath, words in a long forgotten language, the language of witches and magicians.

He was brought back to awareness by calls for help. Smoke was billowing from the cell, so thickly that he could see nothing within.

"Help me!" the girl shouted. "Help me, I'm burning!"

The young soldier jumped to his feet, rushed to the cell, opened it and stepped inside. He was blinded by the smoke. As he stumbled about, trying to find the peasant girl, he felt himself roughly pushed forward and his sword being snatched from his hand. The magical smoke vanished as quickly as it had appeared, and the girl stood before him holding his sword tip against his throat.

"I will not hurt you unless I have to," she said, "but I need your uniform. Take it off and lay it on the floor."

"No," he said. "I can't undress in front of a girl."

Her hand moved faster than he could see, and he felt a burning pain at the side of his neck.

"I will kill you if I have to," she said. "I must have the uniform."

His body trembled and fear came over his face. He put his hand to his neck and brought it back, covered with blood.

"Please don't kill me," he begged. He took off his uniform as fast as he could and stood in his undergarments, shivering and humiliated in front of the girl.

"Go to the back of the cell and lie on your face," she commanded. "I will lock you in. Make no sound. If you call for help, you will be the first to die."

Amara picked up the bundle of clothing, stepped out of the cell, and locked it behind her. Stepping out of her brown

148

peasant's robe, she dressed herself in the uniform. The boy's helmet lay on the floor near his seat, and she put it on. She recognized the uniform as being that of the household guards of the Duke of Intor. Perhaps she was in Intor Castle. Other than that, she had no idea, except that she was all by herself and surrounded by enemies.

The corridor was empty. There was a dim light showing around a bend, so she explored in that direction. Overhead, water dripped from the low ceiling, and the floor was slippery under her feet. Around the bend was a door that seemed to open on a courtyard. She could hear low voices coming from outside.

Perhaps she could cross the courtyard without being noticed. Making sure her hair was tucked securely under the helmet, she stepped boldly out the door and walked determinedly for the first door she spotted on the other side. Out of the corner of her eye, she saw a group of three soldiers lounging on benches against a wall. They paid little attention to her as they seemed to be playing a card game.

As she passed the halfway point across the yard, her luck changed. One of the soldiers looked up and called to her.

"Where do you think you're going, Halmos? You are never to leave your prisoner alone."

She mumbled and gestured to the door in front of her, trying to indicate that she might be going to the latrine. It didn't work.

"That's not Halmos," shouted another one of the men. "She's escaped. After her!"

Amara was trapped. She ran for the door, but was cut off by the guards. She stopped and drew the sword.

"Make it easy for yourself, little girl," one of them said. "Give us the sword and we won't hurt you. The Duke would not appreciate his prisoner being damaged in any way."

"Stand aside," said Amara, pointing her sword at the speaker.

He laughed and stepped forward, drawing his own sword. He struck at Amara's arm, trying to take the sword from her hand. As he lunged forward, she stepped quickly aside and plunged her own sword into his body. She quickly withdrew the blade as the wounded man fell forward onto the ground. The other two men drew their swords and moved to opposite sides of her.

Two against one was not a difficult battle for a trained swordswoman like Amara, whose years of practice with the kingdom's finest instructors placed her several levels of expertise above these ordinary soldiers. She easily dodged their clumsy strokes and, moving quickly away from them, she stepped back in with a stroke to the nearest man's ribcage. Her target screamed in pain, and the other man turned and ran for the door.

Amara followed in hot pursuit, but the guard reached the door ahead of her. She chased him down a hallway and around a corner into a large chamber decorated with crimson wall hangings. At the opposite end of the chamber sat a short, fat man, wearing elegant silver and crimson robes and surrounded by a squadron of armed men. He rose and stepped forward.

"It seems our little sparrow has awoken from her slumbers," said the Duke. "Drop your weapon. You have no chance of surviving if you resist. I think you would prefer to remain alive, and I have my own reasons keeping you among the living."

Amara looked at the troops facing her. Not only was she outnumbered, but these men were trained, combat-seasoned soldiers, not the clumsy prison guards she had been facing. Squaring her shoulders, she laid her sword on the floor. Four men jumped forward and seized her firmly.

"I must apologize for what is about to befall you," said the Duke. "You must be punished for the trouble you have caused my dungeon guards, and I have a use for the part of you that you are about to lose."

The men dragged Amara to a wooden table. As she struggled, they took her left arm and placed the hand flat on the table surface. A soldier drew his sword and held it over her little finger.

"You will not be must troubled by the absence of this small part of your body," smirked the Duke. "If, however, your father does not respond to a minor request of mine, I will be forced to deprive you of larger pieces of yourself, a hand, say, or perhaps a foot."

Amara steeled herself. She would not show fear or pain in front of her enemy. As the blade sliced down, severing her finger from her hand, she couldn't control herself. A loud scream burst from her throat, and the pain was worse than any she had ever felt. Another soldier quickly tied a rag around the stump of the finger to stop the bleeding. Shock set in, and Amara staggered with dizziness. Trying to keep from falling, she blinked back tears and stared at the Duke with fire in her eyes.

"Take the prisoner back to the dungeon," he commanded. "See that she does not escape again. If she does, I will not deal kindly with those responsible."

Amara felt herself being dragged from the chamber. Her struggle to stay conscious failed, and again darkness descended on her.

*

The throbbing pain in her hand, coming from where her finger had been, brought her back to consciousness. She was lying on the stone floor of the dungeon, dressed again in her peasant clothes. She had to regroup her forces. The next attempt to escape must be more successful.

She looked around her new cell. There were no bars allowing her to see anything beyond the solid wood door that was the only exit. Light filtered dimly from a small window high in the wall, far above her head.

First things first. Blood was oozing from the rag that bound her hand. Focusing on the magic spells she had memorized during her years of instruction by the Royal Magician, she concentrated on staunching the bleeding and beginning her healing process.

*

Taran, Asuma, and Rabak stared in horror at the contents of the small wooden box sitting on the table before them in the royal chambers. A small, bloody finger lay mocking them, the accompanying message lay next to the box.

I return part of your daughter to you. If you wish the rest of her returned intact, you must abdicate the throne in my favor within two days. If you do not, every day after_that will bring larger and larger boxes containing parts of your daughter. For her sake, I suggest you act quickly.

                          Your faithful servant,

      Duke Intor.

"The viciousness of that beast is beneath contempt," said Asuma. "He leaves us no choice than to do as he commands."

"Let us not decide in haste," counseled her brother. "Even if Taran should abdicate, we have no guarantee that Intor will release Amara. As long as she lives, the people of Weltoria will recognize her as the legitimate heir to the throne."

"Yes," said Taran. "I think our only choice is to develop a plan for her rescue. We have little time. Let us begin at once."

*

In the dungeon cell, Amara slept fitfully, vivid and disturbing dreams running through her head. Then a welcome sound crept into her slumber.

Far above her head, she heard a cat's loud purring. She looked up to see Shadenni perched on the windowsill high above her. He edged off the sill and ran straight down the dungeon wall to Amara.

"How did you find me?" she asked. "However did you get into this castle?"

153

"I have always been with you in your times of need," said the cat. "I was sent from the world of spirits to guard you until you reach womanhood. The time is approaching for me to leave you and return to the sphere from which I came."

"Why have you never spoken before?" asked Amara, almost speechless with surprise.

"I am not speaking now," said Shadenni. "I am a cat, and cats cannot speak except in dreams. When you wake I shall be gone, but you will remember to look carefully at the path I take when I climb back to the window."

The cat turned and began climbing up the wall. When he reached the window, he paused briefly, purred a farewell, and disappeared from Amara's view.

"Come back, come back!" she cried. "Come back."

"Come back!" she screamed, returning to consciousness. What had she been dreaming about? As if through a haze, she dimly remembered her cat talking to her. What had he been trying to tell her? As she racked her brain, she saw, in the dirt on the floor of her cell, the paw-prints of a cat. They headed straight for the wall and then disappeared. Her eyes followed the wall upward from the prints to the window, high above.

I'm supposed to see something on the wall, she remembered.

Faintly, very faintly, little cracks, finger and toeholds showed themselves to her. It just might be possible to climb the wall to the window. Years earlier, her uncle Rabak had taught her how to scale vertical walls and cliffs. Could she still do it? There was no alternative. She had no intention of waiting in the cell for the duke's next visit.

She started to get to her feet, but dizziness overcame her. She lay back down. The healing spells had begun to work, and the pain in her left hand had been replaced by a dull throbbing. She needed more time. For now, she would memorize the patterns of cracks in the wall, while her body rested for the climb. Chanting the mystical healing song, she drifted back to sleep.

Chapter Three

Kasto sat in enforced idleness in the army's camp in the forest near Intor Castle. Messengers had kept him posted of all developments, including Amara's torture and Duke Intor's demands. He was ready for action, anything to rescue Amara from her captors. He was pacing back and forth in front of his tent when word came that Rabak had arrived.

Kasto welcomed Rabak with great relief. They entered the tent to confer in privacy.

"What is the news?" asked Kasto anxiously.

Rabak repeated the story of Amara's finger and Duke Intor's demand. "We now have made our plan," he said. "Intor will never allow Amara to survive. Her only chance is to be rescued."

He began to outline the plan.

"I will move the main body of our army to the front of the castle," he said. "King Taran will inform Intor that he has agreed to his demands, but needs time to work out the details."

Reaching into his satchel, he removed a rolled cylinder of paper. He unrolled it to reveal a detailed map of Intor Castle. Kasto bent over the map, reading it carefully. Rabak continued.

"Here," he pointed to a point on the outside wall of the castle, on the opposite side from the main entrance. "This is the point where a small force can come closest to the castle walls without being seen. You are to take your twenty of your best fighters and your three best archers to this point, being careful not to be observed."

"They will surely be expecting a rescue attempt," said Kasto.

"Of course," answered Rabak. "But this is our best chance to slip through their defenses."

Kasto listened carefully as Rabak explained. The outside perimeter of the castle walls was patrolled by squads of Intorian soldiers. Each squad consisted of six men, and the squads circled the castle one after the other, about ten minutes apart. If one squad were to be attacked, the next squad would be approaching soon, and would be able to sound the alarm that would bring the entire Intorian force to the rescue.

"This part of the country is dry, so there is no water in the moat," said Rabak. "But the walls are surrounded by a deep ditch whose bottom is lined with sharp stakes pointed upward, which make it impossible to cross."

Kasto nodded. "I see," he said. "If my men can quickly capture one of the squads outside the ditch, we will have almost ten minutes to scale the walls. We can lay a temporary wood bridge over the ditch. But how shall we scale the wall? The top of the wall will surely be well-guarded also."

"This will be most difficult part," replied Rabak. "In my younger days I could have scaled the wall myself and then dropped a rope for you and your men to climb, but I am now too old."

He hesitated, and then continued. "You must throw a rope with grappling hooks on its end to the top of the wall and climb it yourself. Your archers must be ready. When the guards at the top of the wall see the hooks, they will look down and see you. That is when your archers must be accurate. If they fail to hit the men at the top, it will be certain death for you."

Kasto nodded grimly. "Zismelda is here," he said. "And my own archers are the best in the kingdom."

"They will have to be," said Rabak. "You will take five men with you." He then pulled another map from his satchel, this one a detailed map of the interior of the castle. "Here is the entrance to the dungeons. It should not be heavily guarded. Intor's main force will be occupied by our army at the front of the castle.

"This is where you will have to proceed on your own. Our spies have never been to the interior of Intor's dungeons. After you have found and released Amara, come quickly back along the way you entered. If your path is clear, come back over the wall. When you are safely out, our army will begin its all-out attack on the castle."

He handed the map to Kasto and retrieved a leather pouch from the back of the tent. He opened it slightly to show a homing pigeon. "If your path out is blocked, release this bird. When we see it, our army will attack. Find a place to hide until all In-tor's forces have been called to defend against our assault."

Kasto took the pouch from him and looked at the map. Af-ter his years of training and battle experience, he needed but a few moments to memorize every detail. He nodded. "I am ready," he said. "When do we begin?"

"Just before dark," replied Rabak. "We need enough light for our archers to see their targets, and enough darkness for your men to conceal themselves."

*

Deep in the dungeon, Amara returned to consciousness. The pain in her hand had disappeared, and the wound had com-pletely healed. Aside from missing the finger, she felt as good as new, except for hunger pangs which reminded her that she had had nothing to eat since her recapture. As if in answer to her thoughts, the door opened slightly and a bowl of steaming liquid was pushed quickly into the cell. The door slammed shut as quickly as it had opened, and she heard bolts being slid into place. This time she would be allowed no chance to make contact with her guards.

Since the duke apparently did not wish her to starve just yet, he must still need her alive as a hostage. She hungrily picked up the bowl, but the smell coming from it almost made her lose her appetite. Gobs of rancid fat floated on the top of a murky brown liquid. Prisoners' food must come from the piles of rot-ting garbage produced by the castle's kitchens. She needed energy, however. Trying to keep herself from gagging, she forced herself to eat the vile mess.

Shoving the empty bowl into the corner of the cell, she looked carefully at the path of cracks and footholds that were dimly visible in the wall. She remembered Rabak's advice: *Never start a climb until you have memorized all finger- and toeholds and planned your climb in detail. When you're in the middle of climbing a vertical wall, it's too late to look around.* Also, she remembered, moving the head close to the wall could shift the climber's weight away from the wall, with disastrous consequences. Patiently, very patiently, she planned her climb. If she slipped from the wall near the top of the cell, she would have no second chance. The words of the watervoices echoed in her head.

> *In a dungeon's dark hole, a princess's role*
> *Is to strive to regain freedom's flame.*
> *Though sword strokes be made, and magic may aid,*
> *The bride will not be the same.*

Gritting her teeth, she swore to herself that nothing would stop her from being Kasto's bride. She lay back, relaxing her entire body and preparing for her escape.

Finally she rose from the floor. She glanced at the solid wood door. It was intended to prevent her from seeing her guards, but that meant that they could not see her, either. She walked to the wall and began her climb. She took her first finger-hold with her left hand. If the fingers had been weakened by the loss of one of them, now was the time to find out. But they pulled her securely up to the next crack.

Bit by bit, slowly and carefully, she mounted the wall. She tried to keep her heart from beating with excitement as the window came into reach. Both hands on the ledge, toes both in cracks below, her head rose over the windowsill. Now luck was truly on her side. Since the window was so far above the cell floor, no one had felt it necessary to cover it with bars. The opening was unobstructed, and she could see a wall in front of her, across a dusty pathway from the window. Supporting herself on her elbows and forearms, she stuck her head cautiously out the window and looked both directions on the pathway. No one in sight. She wriggled quickly out, onto the path.

She wished to enjoy her freedom, but with no time to rest, she had to decide which way to go. To her right, she saw a door in the wall partway down the path. Carefully erasing her footprints in the dust behind her, she hurried to the door, put her ear to it, and listened for any sound from the other side. All quiet. She tried the door handle. It turned easily, so she opened the door a crack and peeked inside. It seemed to be a storeroom. Boxes and barrels were stacked along the walls and on the floor.

Voices sounded behind her. She slipped quickly into the room and pushed the door shut. The room was almost black, but she found space behind a stack of boxes to conceal herself. She pulled a barrel to close the opening, and stayed as motionless as possible. Outside the door, she heard the voices get louder, then quieter, as they passed the door and headed down the walkway away from her. The first step of her escape had been accomplished, but many more lay before her. She had no idea of where she was in the castle, or how to find a way out. Once her disappearance from the cell was discovered, the entire castle would be searched thoroughly.

For the time being, however, she was free and well hidden. Time to rest and make plans.

*

Darkness was falling fast, and Kasto's squadron, concealed in a grove of trees near the castle moat, was ready for action. They waited in total silence as the sounds of a group of guards came into hearing. The guards were laughing and joking, talking about the rewards they would receive when Duke Intor became king. As they passed the grove of trees, Kasto's men moved swiftly and silently. Pinning their targets' arms to their sides, they thrust gags into their mouths, relieved them of weapons, and bundled them into large cloth sacks. The sacks were pulled back into the woods, out of sight.

Even as his troops were capturing the guards, Kasto, Limlan, and four of his best men dropped a makeshift wooden bridge across the moat. Crossing the bridge, he tossed a rope with a grappling hook at its end to the top of the castle wall. Tugging to make sure the hook had firmly attached itself, he began climbing the rope. Slightly over halfway up, he sensed movement above him. Two men were peering over the top of the wall. One had a sword and was sawing at the rope, while the other was about to drop a heavy stone. Kasto glanced behind him, and saw Zismelda and the other two archers aiming their bows.

Moments later, he had to swing to the side to avoid the body falling past him into the depths of the moat. The other guard was slumped over the edge of the wall. Kasto finished his climb, pulled himself past the guard's body and onto the top of the wall. No other guards were in sight. Evidently the main force of Intor's soldiers was waiting near the front gate, guarding against a possible attack by Taran's army. Kasto signaled to his men below and they quickly ascended the rope, while the rest of his force pulled the bridge and the fallen Intorian soldier out of sight into the woods. When the last man had arrived at the top, Kasto pulled up the rope. The next group of guards to circle the castle would notice nothing amiss.

Below them, in the castle grounds, there was no sign of life. Kasto led his small force down steep steps, bringing the dead guard and the rope with them. Darkness was now almost complete, and they stowed their burdens under the steps, completely out of sight. They were now ready to find the entrance to the dungeon.

*

In front of the castle's main gates, Taran and his army were doing all they could to occupy the attention of Intor and his troops. The drawbridge over the moat was raised and the castle gate looked firmly closed. Taran called into the castle, and demanded to see Intor.

"If any more harm should come to my daughter, I will hold everyone in this castle responsible. Death will be the most pleasant punishment that murderers can expect at my hands."

The gate opened slightly and Intor's voice came from within. "Your daughter is still alive. If you need proof, I will be delighted to supply you with one of her feet, still warm and bleeding. But if you dare to attack the castle, she will die immediately. I give you an hour to withdraw your troops and return to your city.

"The deadline for your abdication has been moved up. If you have not turned the kingdom over to me by noon tomorrow, your daughter will suffer a painful death."

The castle gate was slammed shut.

*

Inside the storeroom, Amara crawled out of her hiding place. The cracks of light around the door had disappeared, and she knew that it must be evening outside. She had heard no sounds from the passage outside for a long time. Carefully, she opened the door and peeked out. At the end of the passageway, a group of dark figures came around the corner and headed her direction. She quickly jumped back into the storeroom, leaving the door slightly open. Muffled voices came from the men approaching her. Why were they whispering in their own castle?

As they drew near the door, she could hear the leader's voice very distinctly. It was one she recognized. When the group came past the door, she stuck out her arm and whispered to Kasto.

"It's me!" she said, pulling him into the room. His men followed him in, and Amara closed the door.

Amara and Kasto hugged each other tightly. He stepped back and held her left hand. The stump where her little finger had been was covered with healing scars.

"I'll see him pay for this," he said. "I've never hated anyone like I hate that fiend."

"The revenge shall be mine," she replied. "I will exact his punishment."

Kasto looked around in confusion. "This isn't the dungeon," he said. "I don't understand. What are you doing here?"

Amara quickly filled him in on her escape. "Where do we go from here?" she asked.

"We were to rescue you from the dungeons, then try to get back over the wall," he told her. He explained the alternate plans.

Leaving the men temporarily in the storeroom, Amara and Kasto stepped into the passageway. A hubbub arose in the direction of the wall, followed by the sound of men running. Their return path was blocked. Kasto took the leather pouch from his belt and released the pigeon.

"For now we shall wait in hiding," he said. "My first responsibility is to insure your safety."

As Amara nodded, he saw a shadow of disagreement pass briefly across her face. He took her by the arm and the two of them returned to the storeroom.

*

Standing in front of their army, Taran and Rabak anxiously watched the sky above the castle. As Taran paced nervously back and forth, Rabak grabbed his shoulder and pointed at the white pigeon flying toward them. It was time for war.

Squadrons of men rolled huge wooden assault engines into place, and heavily armed foot soldiers gathered behind them. Archers drew arrows from their quivers and notched them in their bows. Taran stood behind the engine nearest the castle gate and called again for Intor.

"Surrender now," he called. "You must die, but we shall spare your family and soldiers."

The reply was a barrage of arrows launched from within the fortress.

"Attack!" he commanded.

His archers fired their own barrage of arrows. Under their cover, the siege engines moved forward to the walls of the castle. Barrels of flaming oil poured down from the top of the walls. The men handling the barrels died quickly as Zismelda and the Weltorian archers showed their deadly accuracy. More arrows flew from within the castle, and cries of pain arose from the ground forces as some of them struck their targets.

Zismelda felt a burning sensation, and looked to see an Intorian arrow stuck in her upper arm. She tried to dislodge it, but blood spurted from the wound. She tore a strip of cloth from her cloak, jerked the arrow loose, and wrapped the cloth quickly around her arm to stop the gushing blood. She bent to pick up her bow, but the pain was too much, and she had to withdraw and take cover. Her time in this battle was over.

The assault forces were raising ladders to the walls when a sudden quiet came over the battle scene. No further arrows flew from the castle, no more boiling oil poured down from the walls.

"Halt the attack!" ordered Taran.

As the Weltorian forces waited in silence, a white flag waved from the top of the walls. A man stepped into sight.

"Surrender! We surrender!" he cried.

"Open the gates," answered Taran.

As the assembled Weltorian army watched, the giant fortress gates eased open. The drawbridge over the moat slowly lowered. A delegation of three men, waving white flags, crossed the bridge.

"Duke Intor has fled," their leader said. "Please spare us. We lay down our weapons."

Taran conferred with Rabak, then spoke again.

"Have every man from the castle come slowly across the bridge, throwing his arms into the moat. If all obey, we will honor our pledge to let you live. But if we see any treachery, death will be your reward."

"We accept," said the man with the white flag. He turned back to the gates and waved his arm. One by one, the Intorian forces began leaving the castle and dropping their weapons into the moat.

Chapter Four

From their hiding place, Amara, Kasto, and their small band listened to the battle raging outside the castle gates. When the sound of fighting ceased, Amara and Kasto looked at each other.

"Now we go," said Amara. "I have a score to settle with our duke." She ripped a sword from the belt of a surprised soldier, and before Kasto could stop her, she ran from the storeroom and down the passageway.

Kasto and his men followed closely behind her. The group stopped when they came to the end of the passage and looked out into a large plaza. It was paved with bricks and cobblestones and surrounded by tall, imposing mansions. The square sloped upwards to an even larger and more magnificent building, the ducal palace of Duke Intor. As they looked up the plaza, they saw a small group, led by a fat man in crimson and silver, hurrying in the direction of the palace.

"That's Intor and his lords," said Amara. "My father has won the battle. It's time to collect my debt."

She ran up the street toward the palace, pursuing the duke. When the Intorians heard her footsteps, they spun around on the palace steps and prepared for combat. Amara, Kasto, and their men lined up at the foot of the steps. She pointed to Intor.

"That one is mine," she said. They drew their swords and Intor's men stepped downward to confront them. Hiding behind his men, Intor slipped into the palace and slammed the door behind him. The sound of a bolt falling into place could be heard clearly through the door.

"The coward has deserted you," said Kasto. "Are you prepared to lay down your lives for no purpose?"

The Intorians looked at one another, then slowly laid their swords below their feet and stepped backwards, their hands raised in surrender.

"To the foot of the steps, and lie face down," Kasto instructed them.

As they complied, two of his men stood over them, swords in hand.

"If any of them makes a move, see that it is his last," said Kasto. He led his remaining men up the steps to break down the locked palace door.

Palaces always have small doors in the back for servants to come and go. Intor had trapped Amara while she was leaving just such a door in her own palace. She circled the building to see if she could return the favor. The length of the wall on the right-hand side was solid. As she rounded to the back, she found what she was looking for. Piles of table scraps, thrown into a small alley for dogs to carry away, showed her where the door to the kitchens must be.

The door was partly open. Amara burst through it, sword at the ready. Frightened kitchen servants cowered against a wall.

"Which way to the duke's chambers?" she asked them.

A cook raised a trembling arm and pointed to one of the doors on the other side of the kitchen. Amara rushed through it, down a passageway, through a doorway, and found herself in the same room where she had earlier been tortured by Intor. Across the room she heard sounds coming from a small chamber. She tiptoed to its entrance. When she looked in, she found Intor pulling armfuls of gold and jewels from a chest and stowing them into a sack.

"I'm here to collect my debt," she said.

Intor looked up. Surprise crossed his face, then satisfaction. "How nice of you to give me the chance to revenge myself for the loss of the kingdom," he jeered. Drawing his sword, he lunged for Amara.

She parried his stroke easily and took stock of her opponent. His plump body might be stronger than hers, but he was in no condition for a swordfight of any length. She decided to tease him, to fence with him until he tired.

At the entrance to the palace, Kasto and his men hammered and hammered against the door until it broke loose from its hinges. Leaving the two men to guard the prisoners, they rushed through the entrance hall into the interior of the building. When they came to the main hall, they heard sounds of a swordfight. Kasto crossed the hall and looked into the next chamber. In front of him was Amara, engaged in her battle with Intor.

As Kasto watched, Intor lunged forward with his sword. Amara stepped quickly backward out of reach. Her left foot landed on the jewel sack and she lost her balance and fell. Intor raised his sword to deliver the killing stroke.

Kasto moved forward to help her, and felt himself grabbed from behind. He turned to see Limlan holding him.

"There are times to go to her aid," said Limlan. "But there are also times to let her fight her own battles. Don't deprive her of her vengeance."

Kasto forced himself to remain motionless and watch his fiancée fighting for her life against her archenemy.

Amara rolled safely out of the range of Intor's sword and regained her feet. He was now sweating heavily. His movements were becoming slow and clumsy. Amara toyed with him as a matador toys with a bull. Cuts on his face and arms dripped blood. He lunged at her yet again, and her blade sliced his face from ear to chin. Blood spurted up from this new wound, temporarily blinding him. Amara stepped back.

"I have punished you enough," she said. "I will consider your debt paid. Drop your sword and surrender. Perhaps my father will be merciful when he decides your fate."

The blood dripping from his face could not conceal the hatred that twisted it.

"Never," he snarled, and threw his sword at her. She dropped to the floor to dodge it, and he turned and ran for the back wall of the chamber. Amara sprang after him. A large tapestry covered most of the wall, from floor to ceiling. Stepping behind one end of it, he ripped it off the wall and flung it at her. The weaving fell over her head and shoulders. By the time she could lift her sword and cut her way through it, she saw a low door in the back wall closing in front of her.

Kasto and his men ran into the chamber. Amara sank onto a bench while they tried to open the door by pushing and pulling. It refused to budge.

"There must be an escape passage behind it," said Kasto. "We'll need axes to chop our way through."

By now the main Weltorian army had reached the palace. Amara turned to see her father and uncle standing in the doorway of the chamber. She dropped her sword and walked slowly to Taran. The stress of the past days and the flame of battle dropped away from her, and she became just an exhausted, bone-weary girl, sobbing in her father's arms. Her ordeal was over.

*

That evening, she and Zismelda sat before a fire in the army camp, cooking their evening meal over an open fire. Her father and uncle were dining with their officers in Intor castle, but Amara couldn't face the prospect of returning to the scene of her torture. Kasto's men had been able to break into Intor's escape tunnel, which took them under the castle walls and moat to a small barn in the fields outside the castle. Horse tracks left the barn, heading north, and Kasto had led his men in pursuit of the fleeing duke.

Zismelda's wounded arm was heavily wrapped with bandages.

"Seeing you alive makes all this worthwhile," she said, waving the arm at Amara. She paused. "I think I will need to get better colored bandages for the wedding ceremony. These simply won't match my gown. Do you think light purple would do? Let me see your hand again."

She took Amara's hand and examined it.

"It was kind of Intor not to cut off the finger your wedding ring will adorn," she continued. "You will still be a beautiful bride, even though missing a finger will make you a little different."

Amara smiled. Not even blood and battle wounds could change Zismelda. She started to answer, then froze. The words of the watervoices came back to her.

> In a dungeon's dark hole, a princess's role
> Is to strive to regain freedom's flame.
> Though sword strokes be made, and magic may aid,
> The bride will not be the same.

"Not another person – the same person, slightly altered," she said under her breath.

"What?" asked Zismelda.

"Nothing important," said Amara. "Let's talk about the wedding. I have healing charms that should get your arm back to its natural beauty well before my big day."

*

Much later, the last glimmerings of twilight were disappearing from the sky when Kasto rode back into camp. He dismounted and approached the two young women, who had at last grown tired of wedding plans and were gazing drowsily into the embers of their campfire. They looked up questioningly.

"We couldn't catch up to Intor," Kasto reported. "We followed his trail high into the northern mountains and lost it on the rocks at the summit. Limlan is still trying to track him, but I wanted to come back to be with you."

"Do you think Intor has a hiding place up there?" asked Amara.

"Nothing that we could find," answered Kasto. "I'm sure he's crossed the mountains and entered the lands of the northern barbarians. I don't envy him his fate when they capture him."

The three young people were silent, thinking of the proud Intor doomed to end his life as a slave to barbarians.

"We'll have our spies be alert for any reports of a badly scarred fugitive," Kasto went on. "I personally have already lost interest in Intor's future. I need to concentrate on serving the needs of my bride-to-be." He looked down at the two girls. "We will be separated again until the wedding day. I hope Zismelda will excuse me for what I am about to do."

He leaned over Amara, helped her to her feet, took her in his arms, and held her tightly in a long embrace. Zismelda smiled and turned her head aside. In the depths of the shadows, she could see the glow of embers reflected in the eyes of a watchful cat.

*

Four weeks later, the same cat sat atop a tower wall overlooking the square in front of the royal palace. Puffy white clouds floated in the brilliant blue sky overhead. Trumpets blared to announce the beginning of the day of the royal wedding. The streets of Balarta were ablaze with brightly colored pennants and bunting, which were stirred gently by a light breeze. Smoke rose from fires in the food stalls of the market adjoining the square. In the distance the river, its watervoices silent beneath the surface, flowed calmly through the fields beyond the city.

A raised platform stood in front of the palace. The square was filled with temporary seating provided for wedding guests of all ranks of society. Amara's friends ranged from members of the royal families of all Eight Kingdoms to her oldest friends, peasants who worked in the fields outside the city. All had their special places reserved to attend the ceremony.

Peasants were the first to arrive. They watched in excitement as the nobles came to be seated. Finally, kings and queens and other members of royal families arrived to sit in honor at the sides of the altar. Zismelda's parents, among the oldest and most loyal supporters of King Taran, sat with First Minister Rabak and Kasto's parents in the most privileged seats.

A flourish of trumpets greeted the appearance of Count Kasto, accompanied by Limlan. Kasto looked out at the assembled crowds and smiled at some of his close friends who had traveled far to be present. His good friend Namla, whom he had known since the days of the junior training camp, stood with the visitors from Holunland, next to Lord Damier and his son, Duke Malvane. Once Kasto's bitterest enemy, Malvane had gained maturity in the barbarian wars. Fighting side-by-side with Kasto, he had become one of his closest companions-in-arms. He sent a radiant smile back to Kasto.

Zismelda in her deep pink dress, indeed the most beautiful matron of honor ever, led the final group of participants. Amara and her parents followed closely behind her, to the accompaniment of roaring cheers from the entire crowd. Amara's wedding gown, white with silver threads, shimmered in the sunlight. The pearls woven into her gown and the diamonds in her tiara matched the radiance in her smile as she took Zismelda's arm and stepped to the stage to face Kasto.

As the bridal couple knelt and exchanged their vows, Shadenni, from his viewpoint on the palace wall high above them, purred with satisfaction, even as an un-catlike tear escaped his eye. *From now on Amara will control her own destiny,* he thought. *But if unforeseen troubles should ever arise, I have permission to swiftly return and be at her side.* He rose to his feet, stretched mightily with fully arched back, and relaxed. Pleased with a job well done, he slowly faded from view. No longer visible, he floated through the air, out of the city, across the river, and returned to his home in the world of the spirits.

www.ingramcontent.com/pod-product-compliance
Lightning Source LLC
Chambersburg PA
CBHW030144200626
46812CB00015B/1357